Bène, Carmelo. – Att
matografico (n. Lecce 193
me protagonista del *Calig*
to una compagnia (primo
che ha dato vita a spetta
contro il teatro ufficiale si
lo e uno stile carico di ef
Della sua vasta produzion
tra l'altro la manipolazior
ricordano: *Lo strano caso*
1961; *Amleto* da Shakesp
stra Signora dei Turchi, 1
Marlowe, 1966; *Salomè d*
beffe da Benelli, 1974; *S.*
Pinocchio, 1982; *Lorenza*
Adelchi da Manzoni, 1992
dei Turchi, 1968; *Don Gi*

e regista teatrale e cine-
Ha esordito nel 1959 co-
di Camus e ha poi forma-
o in Italia di anti-teatro),
in cui alla provocazione
iiva il gusto dello scanda-
ti istrioneschi e barocchi.
eatrale – in cui è costante
integrale dei classici – si
 dr. *Jekill e del sig. Hide*,
e e Laforgue, 1964; *No-*
4; *Faust e Margherita* da
Vilde, 1967; *La cena delle*
D.E., 1974; *Otello*, 1978;
o da De Musset, 1986;
ra i film: *Nostra Signora*
nni, 1970; *Salomè*, 1972.

OUR LADY OF THE TURKS

Carmelo Bene

OUR LADY OF THE TURKS

A Novel

Carmelo Bene

Translated & with a preface by

Carole Viers-Andronico

Contra Mundum Press   New York · London · Melbourne

Translation *&* preface © 2021
Carole Viers-Andronico;
Nostra Signora dei Turchi
© 2017 Giunti Editore S.p.A.
Firenze-Milano.
Bompiani, an imprint of
Giunti Editore S.p.A.
First published under the
imprint Bompiani in 1995
www.giunti.it

First Contra Mundum Press
edition 2021.

The translation has been made
possible thanks to a grant
from the Italian Ministry
for Foreign Affairs.
Library of Congress
Cataloguing-in-Publication
Data

Bene, Carmelo, 1937–2002

[Nostra Signora dei Turchi.
English.]

Our Lady of the Turks /
Carmelo Bene; Translated
from the Italian by Carole
Viers-Andronico

—1st Contra Mundum Press
Edition
210 pp., 5×8 in.

ISBN 9781940625492

   I. Bene, Carmelo.
  II. Title.
 III. Viers-Andronico, Carole.
 IV. Translator.
  V. Preface.
VI. Viers-Andronico, Carole.

2021944177

Table of Contents

Translator's Preface

For my husband

My light in the darkness.

TURKS-TOURISTS, SAINTS, & A KNIGHT:
APPEARING AND DISAPPEARING FROM THE ACT

"What matters is that we liberate ourselves from language,
that we concentrate only on its black holes."
— Carmelo Bene, "CB versus Cinema"

To say that Carmelo Bene defies classification would
be an understatement. As an actor and author, he
spent the better part of his life subtracting himself
from the tenets & genres of Western representation
(i.e., tyrannical, conformist power structures) that
he unabashedly despised and ridiculed. Nevertheless,
his rather unique approach to creative production,
infused with an erudition as profound as it was original in its (re)elaboration, left an indelible scar on the
multiple domains in which he (surgically) intervened
during the course of his career: theater, film, radio,
prose, & poetry — nothing survived his artistic fury.

His incursions into such disparate domains may
seem peculiar, if not simply impossible (as he notes
in his "An Autographical Portrait," one life was not
enough to accomplish all he attempted). The breadth
of these endeavors, however, corresponds to a lucid
and meticulously pursued path of research into the
possibilities — and therefore the role — of every do-
main of art. Rather than dealing with representations
and conveying messages — what Bene spitefully calls

the History of (the patronage of) Art — artists should relinquish the constraints of logic *&* the "tyranny of meaning," offering to the witness-spectator only an incomprehensible and thus incommunicable sound-vision experience. According to Bene, the work of art loses its traditionally prominent role to become no more than an empty vessel through which the artist (the real masterpiece) pierces a hole into the fabric of meaning.

The sundry conceptual devices that Bene utilizes in his unorthodox artistic practices originate predominately in his theater. The centerpiece of these devices is undoubtedly his concept of the *actorial machine* — what he defines as "shredding language-representation-subject-object-History." It is Bene's answer to the conventional figure of the actor: instead of performing a role by memorizing a text and parroting it on stage, the *actorial machine* is first and foremost an amplification of the voice, the aural blow-up, or enlargement, of its dynamics and modulations in an attempt to obliterate the image-representation and reinstitute a sort of natural order of things — as Bene reminds us in his "Portrait": "In our physiological adventure [...] the aural precedes the visual."

The *actorial machine* is also the singular instrument that allows Bene to short-circuit the mechanics of representation via the act. In Bene's lexicon, actor originates from the Latin *agere* (imploring, longing for) and therefore the act is antagonistic to the action (in Italian *agire*, or keeping busy): while the action is what belongs to History (i.e., a chronology of intentions, projects, and plans), the act is the eternal present in which the actor is able to lose his "self." In a trance-like state he sheds the burden of representation, of meaning, and ultimately of identity. The subject itself (as Bene emphasizes, the word "subject" comes from the Latin *subiectum*, or slave) consequently disappears. In his narrative version of *Lorenzaccio*, Bene writes: "History is numeration and nomination; it is the historiography of the dead that excludes me. Alive, I am incomprehensible to History; just as History does not concern me."

Since History and representation are deemed suspect, Bene's theater must become a "theater without performance," where all that matters is irremediably on the margins of the scene (what Bene would call, via a play on words, the "ob-scene"). Hence the importance he accords to "un-staging the play": Bene does not proceed by building or adding; his modus operandi is always that of a surgical subtraction. A case in point is his un-staging of Shakespeare's *Richard III*: as Gilles Deleuze points out in "un manifeste de moins," what Carmelo Bene excises from this play are all the figures of power. Only Richard III and the women are left, so that the original tragedy, amputated of its fundamental political core, can become something entirely other: an un-staging echoed in the continuous dismemberment and stripping away of clothing and prosthetic limbs.

The battlefield where Bene's iconoclastic furor is on full display is his filmography (& later in television): four short and five feature-length films directed between 1968 & 1973 made to "demolish the image" via schismatic editing, repetition, overexposed sequences, and hyper-saturated colors. An iconoclasm that also explains his interest in radio and live recitations: the written text was for him only a "deceased oral," and reading was to be intended as "non-memory." Forgetting the written text is the only way to resurrect the oral from the tomb to which writing had condemned it.

The themes briefly touched upon above can be found in his uniquely singular novel, *Our Lady of the Turks* (1966), which Bene describes as "a perverse novel on the *idiolect*" that portrays a "merciless parody of 'interior life,' risibly entrusted to the third-person narrative form: a monody peopled by a thousand and one voices." In Bene's handling of it, however, the novel eschews its pedestrian genre, to favor the phantasmagoric poetry of his protagonist's staged (mis)adventures, rather than a prosaic narrative that captures some kind of quotidian reality. The protagonist does, however, follow a theatrical routine insofar as he uses his quotidian interior space to exercise his art,

with things like imaginary guests and apparitions &
repeatedly throwing himself off the second-floor balcony of his home — extreme pratfalls Bene practiced
in real life.

Indeed, the novel's imaginary characters and apparitions (Turks-Tourists and Saints, alongside Monks
and Priests, and even a Moorish villa) aside from the
many roles Bene himself plays, including a martyr con-
fined to an urn in the Cathedral of Otranto, a candi-
date for sainthood, and a knight in the manner of the
crusaders, are all conjurings in the diegesis that permit him to stage in prose a series of scenarios in and
around Otranto, a place that suffered a gruesome past.

Near the end of the 15th century, the Ottoman Empire waged a campaign in the port town of Otranto in
hopes of eventually conquering all of Italy and con-
verting the Christians to Islam. The Turks invaded in
the summer of 1480 and laid siege to Otranto, whose
inhabitants were either beheaded or enslaved, though
they spared 800 men in an attempt to convert them to
Islam. Given the choice between Islam or death, these
men chose death and became martyrs of their faith.
The siege lasted 13 months before the Turks were defeated and returned home. The martyrs' remains were
later placed in the Cathedral of Otranto, where they
remain to this day.

Since history does not exist in Bene's world, the
siege waged by the Turks in this narrative is outside

of historical time, but it is perpetrated in a particular season. The invaders are the summer Tourists who descend on Otranto en masse. In his autobiography, *I Appeared to the Madonna*, Bene notes that "*Our Lady...* is not only 'an amusing parody of interior life,' a Des Esseintes deflated *&* ridiculed. No sir. It is definitely something else. It is the most beautiful piece, in the form of an historical novel, on my south of the South."

Our Lady of the Turks was (re)elaborated on stage (1966; 1973) and in images in an eponymous film, which Bene calls "a 1968 film, or better yet, the 'anti-1968 film' par excellence [that was] misunderstood to the bitter end."

Much like Bene's autobiography, *I Appeared to the Madonna*, *Our Lady of the Turks* is a statement of method, of a philosophy of art *&* of being, or rather of *not being*, in the world.

This translation project seeks to incite the reader to follow Bene down his deep rabbit hole. A word of caution: there will be no consolation at the end of the journey. Certainly not a happy ending. But instead of a descent or a fall, the reader can expect an ascent, hopefully a levitation. Like San Giuseppe Desa da Copertino, the idiot saint who "went around the world with his mouth hanging open" and who unknowingly flies, terminating his ascensions in the most improbable of places. These impossible and unrepresentable flights of the Saint are the prime example of what

Bene calls "unthinking," which, as Piergiorgio Giacché beautifully explains in his *Antropologia di una macchina attoriale*, is the abandonment that allows the actor to surrender the process of thinking *&* by extension to shed his identity. It is what will enable him to finally offer himself as a pure vision. To simply appear, this time as a martyr, a saint, a knight, and, above all, an idiot.

A BRIEF NOTE ON THE TRANSLATION

This translation is not a repeat performance; it is an "other" performance that attempts its own disappearance from the act. If not always successful in that disappearance, it endeavors to stare into an empty mirror identical to the one Bene embodied. To accomplish this translator's task, the translation often employs unconventional syntax *&* jarring word choices to disrupt the English language and to work on its margins, or its black holes.

To remain faithful to the author's work, and to present Anglophone readers with a similar literary experience to the readers of the original Italian, the translation includes neither footnotes, nor endnotes. There are no explanations given, nor any elucidation provided. There are only black holes.

Author's Introduction

Following the un-writing of the stage, we cannot re-nounce the necessity of verifying the *in-glorifying* of the *auto-actorial body* (apraxia-aphasia) in the exercise (agraphia) of the *typographic body*. Just as the theater is *removed from the stage*, the praxis of writing is also a *removal* from the stage of the page.

If the *oral of the theatric non place* (*&* of the search for the do not wish to find) is *possible* because unrepresentable, the *written* is mere *impossible* representation, because it is already completed.

The *theater without performance* is a *non place* of *author without world*; this *volume* is a *world without author*: author without work, work without author.

The *word before words*, in the dismemberment of the body in Antonin Artaud, is the obsessive laceration and inconsolable loss of *originary unity*. The *automatism* of the *sincere parody* in the *theater without performance* of the actorial machine is a joyful regression into the desert of forms, above and beyond the *before* and *after of the word*, is an inhuman refusal to *express anything*; anti-humanist and anti-artistic, is the breaking of the language *&* of the History of the symbolic cadastre; the tickling blindness of the *inorganic*, crystallized refractory matter subject to the caprices of the mold, in-sensibly veiled by a *nostalgia of things that never had a beginning*.

The theory-praxis of the Artaudian stage, from the idea of the texts to the positively choreographic execution of their performances, was a true failure (Artaud remains in representation), an "accident of the journey" in his painful and brilliant un-writing of the French language, never so *madly* un-thought and tortured, from Rabelais to our squalid æsthetic times. Never was *euro-art* so *rejected*. Despite any authorial paternity, Artaud is his own work vivisected.

My papery incursions are, instead, the umpteenth confirmation of a surgical practice (*antiheroic* and therefore *pornographic*) that, indifferent, tortures painted cadavers (from the revisers of tradition and the neo-avant-garde) of the twentieth-century mortuary; and, in any case, materials dissolved in a shipwreck in a glass of water — splinters glosses detritus — *un-authored, inter-dicted*.

Here you have one example scribbled by he who is a *stranger in his own tongue*:

Our Lady of the Turks (1964) is the *jeu de cartes* of a perverse novel on the *idiolect*. It is an amusing and merciless parody of "interior life," risibly entrusted to the third-person narrative form: a monody peopled by a thousand and one voices.

A setting and a vision of a *south of the south of the saints* (the "homegrown" baroque, the Moorish kitsch of a palace, the cathedral-ossuary of the Otranto martyrs, etc.), "crusts" summoned to feed an ethnic fire... The music is elsewhere.

Our Lady of The Turks

A Novel

To my father

Love me! It's a miracle, you know, it's a miracle that we saved the eyes! Flora, get dressed and go! There was no Flora. Or she got dressed & left. Returning to the mirror: adore me!

Bottles, candles, and chalices of geraniums were smoldering on the table. He let the garments he'd gathered up in his lap fall to the floor, and they were roses. He poured himself a Pernod, 70 proof.

He picked out a top hat, one of the many he used for the theater, and pulled from its depths a crown of thorns. He crowned himself and returned to the mirror.

Turning away from the mirror, he switched on the gramophone: "Amado mio!," played at full blast.

He returned to the mirror again, but only for a second. He walked backwards until he reached the table, all the while observing his image, and blindly felt for the bottle of Antiquary behind him. His hand struck a glass, which he had broken earlier, and wounded him. Immobilized, he felt the blood running down his fingers. He decided to examine it and compare it to the geraniums.

He approached the mirror as a myope and traced with the tip of his bloody finger the essential features of his image reflected there. Only the essential ones.

Like on stage, when he invariably exploited similar accidents. He then placed two candles on the shelves on either side of the mirror and attempted to frame his face within the boundaries of the bloody lines he'd previously drawn, until the contours of his oval were inscribed and coincided. He planned to remain immobile in that position for an hour.

Five minutes later, his eyes, fixed on the eyes, began to water. It reminded him of the interminable conjunctivitis that had afflicted him as a child, and the glasses worn by the ophthalmologists who treated him. He thought back on Des Esseintes and at how mental connections of that kind made his experiment dry up, like drops of water suddenly falling from the ceiling. He wanted to smile, but he did so restrainedly to avoid demystifying the image. He took a step backward, ever cautious, & rummaged around on the table again. He extracted a pair of eyeglasses, which clearly didn't belong to him, and put them on.

Meant for a far-sighted person, they placed him at a significant distance from the reflection. Now he was crying even harder, given the distortion added to the forced steadiness of his vision. He'd think twice before uttering a syllable this time. He hadn't finished putting on his make-up yet. Make-up is meditation. In the end, save perhaps only once or twice, he'd never succeeded in going beyond the preambles in these rituals. He'd lose himself in the ritual, exhausted, wounded, passed out, or drunk, and without grace. Passionate, oh yes! He had, however, chosen to attribute the collapses that precluded him each time from arriving at the final state of madness to his non-method and to his undeniable physical unpreparedness. And he wasn't wrong.

He'd had occasion, in the days that followed his first experiments, to define the prearranged objective madness as a "colorless sum." He'd appropriated the terms *Ursa Major* and *Ursa Minor* from astronomy and used them as basic attributes. In the first, he intended to group together those elements of the ritual that he considered at that point invariable, such as, for example, the geraniums, even if they were withered, the candles, the liquors, the pure alcohol, the ashtrays, the fortified wine, the mirror, thenceforth positioned above the empire shelf. On the other hand, he assigned to the second set of attributes, the so-called variable objects, those that were, in effect, more useful and practical than those from *Ursa Major*, which he destined to an almost perpetual renewal since they were functioning as variants between the officiating chemist and the fixed objects.

In the end, *Ursa Minor* was — he had to admit — one of his weaknesses, because it was a continuous object of distraction. Note that even a cigarette butt was a variant object. That is to say that if, on the one hand, these secondary objects were providing forks in the path and therefore access corridors to the immutability of the fixed objects, by facilitating, for example, with novelty for novelty's sake, the absenteeism of the walls, doors, windows, lateral lights, then on the other hand, however, they were seriously compromising the value of the habit that categorized the *Ursa Majors* as such. Value equals crystallization, an inability to prompt, to communicate, to surprise, to remember, to impart. Ultimately compromising, like when the officiant would attempt to quiet distractions by rambling on, right at the point that the thread of the catalyzing argument had been lost. Not that the classification of the major objects was the result of a choice. It was, rather, something that he endured, such as a quotidian gratuitousness that had been determined by a gesture or a series of extraneous gestures.

In the end, the laboratory as a concept disturbed him, so much so that he'd decided to enter the house, skipping and shouting in falsetto: "Kids, time for dinner! Kids, time for dinner."

And once he'd entered, let's say the room next to the one he'd designated, — pretending to find himself in the latter, but because it hadn't been prepared at all, he wouldn't be able to walk around in there in the dark like he could in the other one; that is, without bumping into things one or two times out of ten, as wouldn't have been the case in the former, — he'd sit in an armchair and begin a conversation, mostly on

Hegel, with an imaginary interlocutor who contra-dicted him. The interlocutor was a dolt who was con-stantly misquoting Marx. Initially, he'd be outraged by him. Then, little by little, the guest would exasperate him to the point of making him swear, shout, insult, and rain curses on him until he finally threw him out.

As soon as he was alone, in the grips of fury and on the verge of tears, he'd find his way to the right room, all the while swearing and slamming doors. In other words, the banality of his predicament would spare him from criticism when he entered the room. Not that this manner of access was indispensable for him, but rather the fact of unleashing a rambling speech in the hall, which he'd sustain until he was drooling, reduced his chances of undertaking another one in his room. Which was a good thing. However, the bile — which was nevertheless equal in volume to authen-ticity — exhausted him more than a little. That was the disadvantage.

Another dangerous disturbance for the grand fi-nale was constituted by a sacrilegious near insult that nevertheless would succeed in catching up with him in the concluding phases, and even confounding him in cracking the combination of his most elaborate and nearly accomplished stupidity. Deconsecration was perhaps the most dangerous agent in the entire exercise, and it could overtake him from all sides, menacing either the propitiatory phase, or the peak of his improvisation, the more unpredictable, the more uncontrollable. Like a tic. The mirror would crack and all would be lost. It was impossible to continue at this point. In moments such as these, which occurred frequently, he'd cover the mirror with an opaque rag, mess up the table, like the altars on Good Friday, and swallow a sleeping pill. This phenomenon would provoke another one that he nevertheless identified with the solution to the first one. He knew he was in the same situation as those suffering from heart ailments, and he felt conditioned above all in the transitions from one decisive moment to the next. He remembered the first Christian rituals, when they would gather in the catacombs, or in the boardroom at the Bank of Italy in the heart of the night. He thought again about the non-official status of his ritual, getting himself worked up with apprehension, so that he instinctively entered into it, without recalling even one of his mental reserves that would preserve this protective measure. The second phenomenon was precisely this state of apprehension which he, nevertheless, ended up preferring to the nightmare of the first one.

It didn't always work, because the tic would sometimes truly surprise him in the nightmare of this precautionary zeal. After all, I'll say it again, he was only successful once or twice in getting within a breath of idiocy.

He sometimes even succeeded in damming up these breaches, for example in the case of this very same improvisation: inscribed in the bloody contours, the crown of thorns encircling his head, controlling his breath so that he wouldn't fog up the mirror's surface, almost in the flames of exaltation, he wanted to overdo it by humiliating himself until it sounded like he was pronouncing the word "province." He stopped at the letter "p," which he kept repeating like a fish. He was trying to mechanize it as to wear out, by practicing his lip movements, the detrimental obduracy of that thought, overindulging in making spit bubbles, ever freer, and then at least one perfect moment. Four seconds at his best: this was his personal record. Not thinking about the word saint four times *&* not even feeling as though he'd been canonized, was equivalent to being a saint for four seconds. The only thing left to do was to gasp for air, while avoiding monosyllables and waiting for the prospect of his divine state, not like for a train or a sailboat, but like for an infernal device capable of obliterating itself in a single burst of flames. The cruelest moment that would've struck him at this point would've consisted in re-making him, creator of himself, the creator of another movement, reduced to an object, even an instrument; in other words, like in nature.

He was also an expert in "communication." But in reality, he felt like he was moving away from his object, which was moving away in its turn and subjectifying itself while changing its role. The state of grace shattered, like a glass just filled, and being no longer perfect, nothing was left to him except opting for that dissolve. Recognizing himself, that is, as an object of his own gesture, at this point autonomous, or proclaiming himself a subject of that autonomy, as in a *memento* and other threats of that kind.

It's true that he almost always resolved to insult a missed opportunity with grimaces — this time by transforming bubbles into spittle — always aimed at the obstinacy that permitted certain of his reflexes to direct themselves and, in any event, to the incalculable detriment of the ardent idiocy which he'd have liked to establish. He'd never boast of his paternity among the insults directed at his failures — he knew the game all too well — rather, he would simply grow sad *&* seek refuge in self-criticism.

Sometimes, he'd even laugh at his experiments. His despondency was mostly physical. He'd feel as though he was being used, like a patient under the knife of a good doctor, and would only complain by changing the subject.

In fact, he was exceedingly courteous during the day, like someone who'd conceived of a great plan. The only thing his nirvana had in common with the times was the Calvary, and most of the time it was only the Calvary.

As it was, in his first attempts at meditation, he'd attributed the failure of his experiments to one or more forms of his complex. For this reason, he'd burdened himself with a disjointed preparatory study that employed phrases like: "For the love of country, let's not talk about social problems," or "I'm a 70-year-old widow," or "Oh, the flower of youth!" and mostly dragging himself on his hands and knees around the balcony. A similar expedient allowed him a state of apprehension equivalent to the one adopted against the danger of the deconsecration. Being no longer troubled by it, he went so far as feeling like a victim persecuted by his complex, a heroic victim, a challenger, who would hide behind invectives like: "I'm not talking to you anymore!" or "It's none of my business!" and other such sayings, up to the point of ending in exuberance & enthusiasm. Not even an elixir, no drug in the world could have decentered him to the point of concealing his limits from him. If he'd been looking for something, it would've been easy to find a surrogate, to replace volume for the idea of volume. He knew that the dialectical method was an arrangement far from the concept of "utility," in the name of which the exposition begins, there where we stop looking for it. We renounce and we amplify ourselves. He'd renounced showing and even expressing himself. He'd renounced renouncing. For this reason, he still mistook his own exuberance as controversy.

But if everything added up, or didn't add up, he'd finally become an idiot. Like a national holiday. Or an authentic idiot. He'd do his utmost to accomplish this with an enthusiasm that only a bank would be able to translate for you.

At times, he'd stop the rehearsal, like an actor — still wearing the crown of thorns — and think of all the idiots in the world. All of them would've willingly traded their own idiocy for the lakes of his failure. It would've undoubtedly been enough to make them into geniuses. Dignitaries of Lilliput & nothing more. So, he'd open his mouth wide in a voiceless scream, &, back in front of the mirror, stretch his lips. Then he'd sing softly, and, as if he didn't want to wake the neighbors, he'd go to the bathroom for the sole purpose of brushing his teeth.

It wasn't that he was particularly concerned about oral hygiene, but rather because he did think it a good thing to take a habit to the point of manic obsession, which he considered the rhythmic gymnastics of deficiency. Then he'd return to the mirror.

At times, he couldn't hold back from congratulating himself. During the breaks — not while resting — for example, which is why he'd give encores at the expense of the rhythm. Keep in mind, it was always a matter of fractions of seconds. All of his blanks were imperceptible in the end. Another theatergoer, whoever that may be, wouldn't have had time to even

applaud him. The exceedingly emotional approval —
when that was the case — of a fervent spectator would
always reach him a moment later, when, with the se-
quence already compromised, he'd think that he was
distracted by something else. At that point, he'd stop
abruptly, attributing the interruption to the excitement of that uncontrolled participation. This gave him
the impression of being dishonest, like saying "I know
my audience!" By going on a tangent in this manner,
he'd get excited and threaten to pack his suitcases.

During these interruptions, he'd allow himself a
little break, which was almost always filled with drinking whiskey and speaking loudly, but politely, as you
would at a party. The sorts of phrases that he most often used smacked of things like, "I disagree!" or "Let's
get out of here!" or other polite expressions lacking
in good manners of that kind.

All of a sudden, he'd go back on stage. That evening he
rummaged around everywhere. He extracted a cross pen-
dant &, approaching the mirror, looked at himself in it
as if looking around the room. The framing didn't permit
him to see beyond his throat. He was holding the cross
in his left hand. He tried to put it in his right hand. Then
he put it in his pocket. He felt a shudder, &, in the space
of a second, opened the door to the balcony. He closed it
gently, and leaned against it obliquely like a blind man,
trying very hard to convince himself that there was
someone on the other side who wanted to force it open.

He returned home late that night. It was well after the clock had struck midnight. In order to conquer his determination, he slipped inside, as usual, by quickly ridding himself of his nonexistent companions. He mumbled courtesies, such as: "I owe you one!" or "Where did the time go? It's getting late!" or even "I really need to go to bed!" He turned on the light in the hall, and then feigned a start, as if he'd suddenly found himself facing an unexpected individual, an accomplice, and said a little too tersely, "You, here?" He lit a cigarette. "All right. I'll be ready in exactly one hour, just the time it'll take to pack my suitcase. In the meantime, you're welcome to take a nap on the couch!"

He went to his room, closing the door behind him nonchalantly. Here, out of sight, he turned the lock in such a baroque manner that the accomplice, even the most *real* one, wouldn't ever have suspected. He lit a candle, one in the corner. Using electricity would've startled him. He walked toward the window. It was closed. He closed the shutters as well. He pretended to look at the street. He was also gesturing with his arms, perhaps signaling, but he stopped as soon as it seemed they'd been understood. He poured himself a cognac and knocked it back.

Oh, Margherita! He remembered her in a flash, as if a loved one in danger. He should've made it up to her. He'd caused her sorrow and was about to do it again. He had to make it up to her. Also, because it wouldn't kill her. All he needed was an impertinence. He flew to the garden where the lights were off. He avoided the flowerbeds with the geraniums *&* raced to the rosebush that ran along the perimeter wall. He ripped up all the roses. Little white roses. He covered himself in cuts. He began biting himself and sucking on his fingers. He could tell his fingertips were bathed in blood. He hesitated for a moment, but then returned to the roses, this time gathering them more carefully, all the while repeating annoyedly, "I got it; it's all right!" He counted them. 23. At least in the dark. He tiptoed back up the stairs. When passing through the hall, he remembered to remember his guest, the accomplice sleeping on the couch. He decided that the guest was, indeed, sleeping *&* went to his room. He also remembered that he was bleeding. He switched on the light. It was worth it. He placed the flowers on the table and examined his hands. In fact, there were red drops on the extremities of two or three of his fingers. He looked at himself in the mirror and closed his eyes. Then he ran bloody fingers at random all over his face. He succeeded in smearing blood on his forehead, his nose, and his chin. He didn't hear anyone knocking, and this made him think of the lily lashes on the windowpanes, there on the balcony, when the weather was bad. He would've liked to write something that started with: "Oh, if then!..." And what was it that he was intending to do with those roses?

Then he'd slowly don a surgical gown. Dressed in this manner, he'd unmake and remake the bed, tucking in everything, even the top sheet. After that, turning anxiously to no one in particular, he'd say: "I'm sorry!" He'd free himself from the surgical gown, after pausing for a moment, and go to the mirror. He'd mess up his hair mumbling in a distressed state: "Why! Why?" answering himself hesitantly, as if he were being interviewed, in French. He wanted to appear on the balcony, as if a crowd were clamoring for him, to thank them, but the latch was rusted. It wouldn't slide without making noise, so he gave up.

He had the impression that it was daytime. He looked at the clock in the drawer. It was one o'clock in the morning. He imagined that it must have been ten o'clock outside, and he heard the band playing.

Goodbye Margherita! We say exaltation, don't we? Or is it like when we swim in the sea while it's raining, or not?

Now the band's music was much louder, as if right outside his windows. One day, the idea of her would kill him. The band's racket saved him from having to say "Who's calling me?" or "Come in!" if they knocked, or drowned out the ringing of the non-existent telephone, and if it were to ring that would be worse.

He was annihilating himself extremely close to the mirror's surface. He was washing his face with alcohol, without drying it off & terrifying himself by threatening to caress the flickering candles' flames sparked by the drops falling from his face. Now the band's racket was deafening, as if they were playing in his room, and his heart contended by strumming. The threats were minor threats.

In a spasm, he decided to raise that soundtrack's volume, yet again, and superimposed applause on it. This was the easiest sound he could conjure up, because it was always there, this crowd lurking in the shells of his ears. He deserved a standing ovation that night. He took advantage of it immediately in this way: the sound of the slaps dominated; oh, if only it were a definitive punishment! If only she were to take offence & leave for good! "So, take that, whore! It's over!" To avoid a scandal to boot. At that very moment, Saint Margherita appeared to him. His own terror gained level after level, when the image of the Saint, the sweetest saint, was moving around the room as if being pulled along on ball bearings, mistreated by the fervor of the faithful, all of them miraculously healed, and to him she repeated like a broken record, in a perfidious celestial articulation: "I forgive you; I forgive you!"

This was when the scandal began. He gathered all the money in the house and threw every bit of it out the window. And the band was playing "Amado mio!" It played for him, who by then had nothing left except an attempt at indecency. He undressed &, completely naked, gave in to a fit of rage, including insults.

At this point, the Saint was no longer standing; she was in bed, curled up under the sheets, all the way up to her neck, where she was smoking and leafing through a women's magazine.

He was on all fours, on the floor, under the bed, flailing around while imitating a pig's oink. He came back to himself when he heard the gramophone's needle skipping beyond the grooves. He was ashamed of himself and wanted to punish himself further when he heard the neighbors complaining. He threw on some clothes. Now it was truly daytime. He ran down to the street and, with thanks, he had the astounded street sweepers return as much of the money as they'd been able to recover with their hands.

He went back up to his room, poured himself a Pernod, and started to write: "And the band was playing 'Amado mio!' It played for him, who by then had nothing left except an attempt at indecency. The Saint was no longer standing; she was in bed, curled up under the sheets, all the way up to her neck, where she was smoking & leafing through a women's magazine."

He chose not to sleep. He was a little worn out. This would be favorable for his state of absurdity. It would've been more prudent to anticipate a collapse. He thought about his stimulants.

He opened the closet and resolutely pulled out a flag, the Italian one: white, red, and green. Just looking at it raised his hackles. It was decidedly the combination of colors that did it. Not that he was allergic — he wasn't allergic to anything — on the contrary, he'd chosen carefully, once and for all, the objects that provoked him, predominately adopting precisely those that left him entirely indifferent. In this case, he was fairly far from a national polemic. It was the opposite; what infuriated him about that object was its extreme indifference. Then he was full of envy, so much so that he shed tears for it. That morning he cried more than ever.

All his extravagance was merely a detox treatment. The starting point of his nightly routines and that of his therapy were only a single moment. The alcohol abuse didn't harm him.

He'd stopped crying a while before. He drank a cup of tea and slept. Recently, he was able to rest. He'd also started a detoxifying treatment for his liver, Laevocistein, that was administered to him intravenously every other day. Not that it helped all that much, but it did of course weaken him. That's how he was able to rest.

He'd sleep. When he was tired, he'd sleep with his mouth open. Like an idiot. It would've made him happy to know that. He would've passed his nights by watching himself sleep. After all, life is essentially being present at either a calamity or a party, but only being present, involved up to a certain point; at best, we are witnesses & nothing more. The weight is religion, ethics, and oftentimes æsthetics, lead roses and heavy clouds, blankets of snow. You need only create a vacuum, stop relying on your muscles, stop walking because you have legs. Fly. Be present. Be present with your whole soul, look with your whole soul. Become impassioned as if for someone else's circumstances. Be ashamed of your own problems. Indulge yourself. Be nice to yourself. Where you find a prison, free a butterfly. Kill one instead of leaving. Fly. Sleep. Fly while asleep, to love without being loved, or even love reciprocated. Above all, decide when it doesn't depend on us, and, if it does depend on us, obey. In any event, sleep. Or simply fake it.

Certain afternoons he'd leave the house and the town and head toward the sea, but steering clear of the small roads. He'd cross the fields of thatch and thorns, weak or irrational, we don't know to what extent. He'd go into raptures over snails. The breeze would pass close to him, like a young woman with uncombed hair in those dead hours, unhoped-for, a memory in foliage from plane & chestnut trees, carob and wild honey, milk, a daughter of the morning, and a daughter of the evening, wonderful and joyful, an aria in the musical sense, as colorless as a blessed life, which is lived only because we talk about it or because we talked about it, impossible. She passed close to him as if by chance, involuntarily blowing on the wings of dead butterflies, as invisible as gold & the heat within the emerald sea.

And him, bewitched as if turned to clay, scantily dressed, painted who knows when, with his hot blood still coursing through it, like in a disregarded miracle, perhaps yet another amphora of wine, abandoned in the shrubbery by ancient Athenian peasants on a feast day, where there were plane trees, chestnut trees, and arbors of purple and of shade, and there wasn't yet shrubbery. Today, felicity of fatigue, far thornier than the amnesia of his own fatigue of felicity.

And suddenly he returned, human up to the point of enslavement to his afternoon, a water carrier, like any other, carrying hot water all the way to the shore, the end of the adventure and of the fairy tale, exhausted from the wild clumps of earth and not the waves. Face down against the froth of the azure sea, like an overturned amphora, renouncing its contents for the integrity of the receptacle.

He imagined that someone passing by on the path in the distance greeted him, and he returned the greeting with a wave. See you tonight. But like that, without saying when exactly. And, once evening came, he decided that it didn't matter.

"I cannot," he thought, "renounce losing you, just as I cannot lose you, Margherita!"

At this point, he'd call out his name loudly and immediately obey, as if there were no time to lose. The sooner he ate dinner the better. He'd make his happy way toward home, imagining himself to be famished.

Before going in, he'd check his mailbox. There was never anything there. Nobody knew his address, but he'd always find a letter there nonetheless. That night, what's more, the news was disconcerting. Complete craziness. And he went in. He decided against preparing himself a Martini. He crossed the hall mocking himself and repeating: "I don't have time for this!"

As soon as he was in his room, he looked out over the balcony on the shrubbery and the violet sea. And there were so many stars. He leaned against the parapet and wished that the first street lights would come on, & for his mother to be calling for him. He amused himself by not responding. Then he sighed, promising himself that he would go, without fail, to the city the following day on family business.

Back inside, he decisively attacked a bottle of laxative, Eparema, which was empty, forcing himself to suck the impossible. He sat down and started to write: "My dear," when he heard someone calling from the courtyard. Nobody. Any pretext to cross the hall in a hurry.

As abruptly as usual, he'd shatter the fiction and flop down on a chair, like an unnailed crucifix. This humiliation of discouragement was, in the end, the most benevolent and compassionate aspect of his failure, which cut off one of his wings and not the other. One wing for his ecstasy, like when we limp while flying, and the other, the active one, only the wing of perseverance. But oh, the unbelievable epiphanies, saints who saw their own wonders reflected within the panes of the most crowded mosaics, documented because alive, to come, Madonnas for whom they had laid down their dreams of woman truly dreamed, to whom, once awoken, the saints had considered and never promised: "I want to live with you forever!" Bronze roses, perfumed with incense, without the escape of a reference, indescribable like life made into ritual, like the party when it was joyous, asleep while praying for sleep, dreaming the very dream that they were praying for. Monks who during the day were busy in a pigsty, and who would fly at night, as clear as faith, because believing only their own eyes, without eyelids, ecstasies. Idiots for more than a moment, capable of resuscitating a dead man but not capable of hurting a fly, eternally incapable of spreading rumors, thoroughly prepared for miracles as long as they don't give you any details.

God God! God's name is made from two names! For saints it's different: their names are made from two attributes. He thought about his first and last name. That's definitely not enough to become a saint, but it is sufficient to make you an idiot.

Invoked and obtained, his sleep was nevertheless cut short. His ultimate idea of her would overtake him, but like a consecrated wind traversing the altars, reaching him without even so much as a breath, like a feather falling on a still lighter sleep. So, he'd pretend to be dead. That wouldn't matter anymore if it was for love. Dead, dead, murmuring to himself: "You were mine, you were mine, you were mine!" White and light blue feathers like moonlight on wounds. Green feathers, as if beneath an even lighter moonlight. Red ones, like a story of a crucifixion, but a slow-moving story, without wind, leafed through, like a May rose on a very pleasant night, one feather after another, painless, like the emotions of every heart that heard that story. A paradise of feathers.

On the starriest night in August, while on a road whitened by dust and not by snow, Saint Martino lent his evening cloak to a man who had just left his plow. The half-naked farmer accepted the knight's gift, like someone who is dying in summer and thinking back on a wintery luxury that he was never able to enjoy. That regret was also a fiction. The knight was a saint armed in iron, charitable, and his cloak was a snowfall on his faith of iron. The man accepted the gift because he'd been taught charity, but only in the name of the image that, undoubtedly, like the knight, would've soon covered him in snow. August snow. Soon. And he, unlike his knight, would've felt it, like one who obtains peace from one who brings peace, returning home among the slumbering flowers, stealing cherries from the unfrozen cherry trees, and then covering himself in a happy sleep. As soon as winter came, he'd give that cloak to someone much less fortunate than himself, perhaps because at Christmas, according to another image, that cloak would've become dust. This man, however, was not made of iron, and moreover the weather was unbearably hot. He left his cloak in a field and made his way homeward, telling himself over & over again that he wasn't an ingrate.

He was playing dead. This was around three o'clock in the morning, and he was imagining remarks, such as "Who would've thought?!" He put himself in the shoes of all the survivors. Until half past three. At that time, sure enough, the geese in the neighboring garden would start honking. The first time it happened, he thought it was coming from a sawmill. So, then he'd imagine that he'd already been buried, but almost always ended up feeling like a good-for-nothing. He was looking at the face of his benefactor who, after bringing him back to life, was reprimanding him: "Get up and run!" At three in the morning. So, he rose like a snake and cleared the table of the geraniums, candles, & bottles. It was a night without illusions &

without moonlight. He also deprived himself of *Ursa Major*. His table became a sky without suggestions. He started running around the table, trying to catch up to himself, after having imitated his benefactor's voice, shouting: "Stop him!" Turning around the table, more and more frenetically, he became distracted by *Ursa Minor*, which was constituted at that moment by the unmade bed and by the many cigarette butts on the floor. He stopped in his tracks, and, in a flash, turned off the light. He resumed running, still going round and round in an incredible manner, while tearing up his hips on the corners of the table, stumbling in *Ursa Minor*. The geese were honking more & more loudly, screaming in his throat. He was running, wounded, and justifying himself to the crowd of an imaginary circus every time he fell.

Outside, it was daytime, with the sun high in the sky. Pointless to have turned off the light. He came to a standstill, all the while breathlessly persuading himself: "It's nothing!" He tried to find the balcony with his swollen, black and blue eyes, searching around between the luminous slits and attempted to open the latch with what little strength he had left. He finally threw open the door and found himself bathed in sunlight. He closed his eyes. He remembered how high it was, nearly the length of the whole second floor, and climbed over the parapet, holding on tight, while pretending to call out: "Help!" Then he let go and fell to the street. He landed painfully on his butt. It wasn't the first time he'd thrown himself out the window. No one came to his aid. He was black and blue all over and bleeding, especially from his forehead. He looked around *&* remained motionless, lying on the ground, until he saw, or at least thought he saw, some people coming his way in the distance. He tried to stand, but it was difficult for him. Nevertheless, he dragged himself toward the steps, always persuading himself: "It's nothing!" On hands and knees all the way up the stairs, if he could've been certain that no one would notice him, he'd have liked to start running. Since he was unable to do so, he dragged himself along while singing softly. He passed through the kitchen, where he washed his face, and then crossed the hall, surprised to find no one there. As soon as he was in his room, he looked at himself in the mirror. He reconstructed everything that had happened in his own way, threatening: "This time, I'll press charges!" He had time, 24 hours, and he closed the door to the balcony. He found his bed *&* lay down on it, aching more than ever. He got up, lit a candle, and ransacked the room. At long last, he pulled a ream of paper stamped for official documents in the order of 200 lira out of a drawer and started to write: "After what I did, et cetera!" He signed it, folded it in two, and sealed it in an envelope on which he put a stamp. Then he ran to the kitchen as if the coffee was boiling over.

Not at all. He went back to his room and feverishly reopened the envelope. He read it somewhere between bored and ministerial and observed: "They're all the same, they're all the same!" and he threw it in the trash.

Then, on certain nights, when he was ready for anything, and before starting his routines, he'd take out his passport from a drawer and place it on the center of the table, ostentatiously visible from every angle of the room. In extreme cases, this object would be the most important among those in *Ursa Major*, the stability of the fixed objects, along the lines of a polar star. It wasn't that he feared the police would unexpectedly burst in on him: the carabinieri would lower their heads, embarrassed, if they happened to pass him on the street. "What's in a name?" That document was completely foreign to him, just like all the other objects from *Ursa Major* for that matter. These were established by the communal, quotidian sun and not by him. He'd only see to the variants. He'd place his passport on the center of the table. Just seeing it there would reassure him, like a rose is the month of May's alibi, even if you don't like flowers. He'd do it so no one would bother him. He'd deduce the month of May from the braying of the donkeys. The others from the scents. But, that document was simply a social convention, and for that reason it left him indifferent, indifferent enough to make him furious.

In his most elegant performances he'd put it in his jacket, in the interior pocket, close to his heart. Then, when at the apex of all the excitement, alarmed by his very own sensitivity, feigning a promise, he'd hold his hand over his heart to control its beating, that envelope would constitute a sealant, compromising his ability to control it. He'd dress himself to the nines only when he planned on going a great distance. Any old card with his name on it would've been essential for him. Nor, however, would it ever even occur to him to inveigh against the objects from *Ursa Major*, but against the fixity of the polar star, oh yes.

He'd have to accept the state of his heart. He'd grow nervous and pull the passport from the depths of his pocket and then throw it out the window. However inconceivable, he'd almost simultaneously run down the stairs to pick it up on the cobblestones. Then, he'd return to the balcony, toss it onto the street again, and then rush down to pick it back up again. This an infinite number of times. Dripping in sweat, he'd decide the game's outcome randomly, to challenge the collapse that could mesmerize him, either in the act of throwing the object out the window, or in the moment of recovery. Most of the time, he'd lose his strength just after the recovery. Sometimes, the object wouldn't make it over the balcony, perhaps by getting stuck in the iron grating. Be that as it may, he, being resolute in ignoring his own clumsiness, would rush down the stairs, search everywhere, on the street, behind the hedge, until it was clear that it was pointless. He'd ultimately fall into despair and start to cry. Luckily, he'd go back up to the balcony to throw himself off it, and, in this way, would find his document, simply lying there on the balustrade. Then, he'd put it in a drawer, but under lock and key.

Other afternoons, he preferred going up to the terrace, high above the palm trees, and a great deal higher than the sea. He'd go up there via the dilapidated external staircase that looked more like a fresco of a staircase than one you could climb, while holding a glass of milk thistle B12, with the confidence not of a guide, but rather of he who is guided, turning around from time to time, but irritated by the throngs of people following him and expecting him, at this point very high up, to speak, even if only a single a word. With his head turned over his shoulder toward the crowd, inspired, and with eyes closed, in fact he experienced only dizziness, he intended to clarify, first and foremost his position to the crowd. They'd go to the terrace, he'd be responsible for that, but they wouldn't have the right, in any case, to misinterpret him. To that end, he would repeat at every step: "Not this one!" Once he'd arrived at the top, had the staircase been made of wood, he'd have kicked it, or have poured jets of tar, boiling oil, or urine on it, but then they'd have seen him.

Better to have them climb up and organize a jumping competition. Was it a Roman settlement, or not? The fact was that the euphoric crowd, little by little, would move closer and closer to the parapet, and then jump in groups onto the cobblestones below, as if the house were on fire. In the end, bewildered, he'd hurry to try to save at least one. Then he'd look down at the street in shock, murmuring: "What kind of madness is this!"

The height that separated him from the cobblestones was at least three times greater than that of his balcony. Having calculated *&* experimented it many times himself, he never would've attempted it. He involuntarily knocked over his glass of medicine and covered his ears so that he wouldn't hear it crash on the street. He heard people shouting and swearing at him down below; undoubtedly people, family members who had turned up to gather the remains of their dead, and that he, without wishing to, had struck.

He'd wander around on the terrace like a survivor. It was an August sun. So, he'd wrap himself in a white sheet, one from the many that had been hung up to dry. He meditated again on the massacre, on the unprecedented barbarism of that deadly euphoria, a people who were undoubtedly unprepared. No doctrine in the world would ever have rendered him the author of a foolish thing like that. Everything was in the method. Like, for example, when he wanted to deceive his vertigo, he'd go down the length of the fresco of his staircase as quickly as possible while thinking about crying out: "Thief! Thief!"

As soon as he was back in his room, he'd start to reread his diary. Every so often he'd raise his eyes and, as if to discourage his therapy's strangeness, he'd go off the rails proffering hasty opinions, such as: "The longer the game lasts, the more you discover!" or "I'm sorry to disappoint you!"

He'd think of other things. When nothing came to mind, he'd mutter poems. For example, "Near the cradle in a gentle act of love," was one of his favorites, since he never could remember how the rest of it went, starting with the second verse. So, he'd repeat the first one over and over again, now softly, now shouting like a man possessed, raging against objects, books, notebooks, chairs, until he managed to destroy everything in the room.

As soon as he was certain that he had lost all trace of reason, he'd become himself again and do his utmost to repair the damage the best he could. He was thoroughly equipped with tools, duct tape, mastic, even for porcelain. He'd busy himself with it until evening. During this second effort he'd sluggishly repeat some verses again, preferably one from the same lyric poem that had discomfited him before, but this time it would always be the last verse so there wouldn't be a need to remember what followed, only peace, a certain satisfaction, as if he'd recited it from start to finish from memory.

Thus, he'd repair the furniture and pick up the books and the broken pieces while repeating "you'll be able to rest." During this process of restoration, it would always seem to him that his father was there to give him advice, and he'd agree with him drearily until he'd hit a finger with the hammer and then shout: "words of wisdom!"

When everything was back in order, he'd mop the floor. Then he'd dress himself to the nines and go outside via the kitchen, closing the door behind him. He'd hurriedly run down to the shed in the courtyard, where he'd retrieve a pair of crutches, go back up the stairs, deftly managing his reentry on those pieces of wood, but this time via the front door. He'd cross the hall, and, once at the threshold of his tidied-up room, he'd rest for a moment on his crutches, satisfied, pronouncing loudly in an encouraging tone, loudly so that a whole factory could hear him: "Well done, well done, well done!" Upon which, grandiloquent, he'd make his way to the balcony, clearing his voice and smiling subtly. At the balustrade, looking down below, he'd see many people one minute and then no one. He'd have to give a speech. He was torn, not because he was panicking, but from the desire to throw himself down there. This temptation had become one of his tics. He'd resolved to defend himself from it by rationalizing the frequency of his public relations, without, however, reducing that frequency. Enjoying a little break and liberating himself from the crutches, he'd remove himself from the balcony and gain, via that fresco of a staircase, the terrace with some apprehension, in any event, regarding the excessiveness of that break. Once reaching the parapet, he'd listen to himself like an orator gifted with myriad methods, or comforted by the principle that, from up there, the only conceivable thing was a mass suicide. And his manner of recitation would renounce the lyric in order to assume, in exchange, the most meticulous tone of analysis, undoubtedly protected from the synthetic possibilities of the second floor. From up there he could recount and diffuse everything that he didn't pay for, and simultaneously in an extended manner, without it becoming an object of any psychosis. The Angelus bell would ring, and the crowd wouldn't have any intention of going home, so as not to miss a single word from him. So, he'd begin a sort of refined rosary. He'd humbly say: "good evening," and the crowd would respond to him equally humbly in kind: "good evening." He'd always have to abandon that rosary prayer to a certain mystery, seeing as how his emotions would compel him, under the pretext of getting down on his knees, to back away from the parapet. And always when night came.

He'd climb down that sketch of a staircase in the grip of an ordinary terror, which is why, when faced with an obstacle, he'd say over and over again: "I'm not worthy, I'm not worthy!"

He went into the kitchen and was about to brave the hall, but his gaze collided with the calendar hanging in the corner; it was a very up-to-date ecclesiastical calendar. His heart started racing, because it was, in no uncertain terms, that very day that the bishops were meant to meet at his place to decide on his saint-hood. Their animated voices and the rustling of their garments confirmed it, along with all the regalia of gold and the blazing red in the frame of the closed door at the end of the hall, or set as if a diamond, and a topaz, and a ruby in the empty keyhole. Evidently, those scholars hadn't locked the door; they knew he wouldn't have dared to enter the room where they were holding their council.

"I've been waiting for centuries, best to wait anoth-er whole year in the kitchen, otherwise who knows when it'll come up again," that's right, that's what any-one else would have thought in that moment.

It was a delicate experiment. All the saints were invariably dead when their state of grace was exam-ined. He, on the other hand, was more alive than ever. If nothing else, he should've had the modesty to ab-sent himself on that occasion. He should've done so, at least for modesty's sake.

He should've waited outside. Those venerable old men would've read his diary from beginning to end. Of course, his writing wasn't always easy to decipher; it would've been better if he were to read it aloud to them and then maybe he would've withdrawn at the time of the council's decision. But at this point it was too late; he should've been in his room before they arrived. How was it possible that he'd forget such an important date? He went down to the street slowly. The red moon was wounding itself in the shrubbery and then bathing in a sea of blood. The balcony windows were open. Walking on his tiptoes to the middle of the street, he'd watch the red vapors rise and then fade into gold and silver, like the inside of a vault adorned with frescos. They'd inform him with a wisp of smoke when it was time for him to come back up.

It started raining, at first a warm rain, and then a much colder, pouring rain. Luckily, he had his raincoat with him, a faded British raincoat that he'd wear even on sunny days. He was simply standing there, soaked to the bone, like any other Enrico, mindful that, in the meantime, up above an altar was either being prepared or cleared away for him.

They would've made him a saint. It was raining even harder. They would've made him a saint, he who wanted to become an idiot. Indeed, all the saints had left their small towns to lick the gold of the pontificate throne, perhaps for the opportunity to spit on it. "God sees you": in childhood, a warning, then growing up: "if they come to understand."

They would've made him a saint. They had come to understand. He'd have to stop it. But how? He'd have to halt the council proceedings. Present his excuses. Explain to those fathers that there had been a misunderstanding. Maybe they wouldn't have believed him and taken such a revelation as considerable proof of humility in grace.

They'd have transferred him to Rome.

He had to stop that council. It was still pouring rain. Perhaps he'd gotten the date wrong and that was why he'd decided to imagine this event today. It wouldn't have changed anything, it would still be tomorrow. He'd need to confront it, escape it. He was soaked to the bone from all that rain. In truth, he was pretending to wait while trying to find a solution. "Yes, that must be it," he'd had a fit, he'd dreamt up the whole council to avoid going home. He was afraid of that balcony of his. He'd chosen an event that would occupy his place for several hours. He'd have taken a little trip, even to the next town over, while up there they'd be discussing his glory. It was raining too hard. He should've gone back inside, if only for a moment to prepare a bag, even a very light one, but go back inside. Disturb all those old men, bother them by opening the closets, the table's drawer, and once this tactful pretext was established, he could also have decided not to leave, and instead direct them to the closest hotel, and go to bed. It would've been better to confront them, to explain to them why he'd chosen the everyday over ecstasy. He decided to burst in. He was in his room in the space of a second. Useless to describe the scandal. He couldn't distinguish anything, except burning candles above a red altar. He cleared a path between the gold and the silver all the way to the table. He seized possession of his diary and locked it in the closet. Misunderstanding an attempt at humility, exactly as he'd suspected, when he turned around, those priests were all prostrate at his feet. No doubt about it. They had made him a saint. "Reverend sirs," he said, stammering while pouring himself a drink, "it's all a mistake. It's pointless to force me to go through the trial of the demon," he added when he noticed that they weren't getting up. He recited two or three blasphemies as proof of his perversion. They were still on the floor with their heads bowed. He blasphemed again, and this time in a deplorable manner. They weren't listening to him. They were adoring him. It was dogma. They had made him a saint. As it was, his immunity annoyed him, like when he'd throw himself off the balcony without suffering any consequences. But this time it was eternal. He'd have liked to find a way to counter it, an expedient that would be equivalent to saying that, "he would show them." Still plodding along between the red, silver, and gold, he got up on the table and improvised a frenetic dance. The bishops crossed themselves.

He started to insult them with obscenities, and those fathers, noting how much dust that saint would force on his own pride, they, too, would castigate themselves by hurling unspeakable insults back at him. At this point, it was mayhem. "They shouldn't have done this to me," he said crying. Seeing that their faith was unshakable, indecency was pointless, so he attempted to fly from the flat surface of the table to the bed. He missed the edge and fell backwards. Having soared in the manner of angels, what followed was a ruinous fall that earned him a broken leg. He dragged himself on all fours toward the medicine cabinet, pulled out a bandage that he then soaked in whiskey & wrapped up his right leg from his foot up to his thigh. He laid down on the bed under the sheets, adopting an extreme, raspy, and compromising tone, saying: "There are idiots who have seen the Madonna, and there are idiots who have not seen the Madonna."

"I'm an idiot who has never seen the Madonna." Then, he sat down on two pillows, leaning against them, with no small effort, & continued: "Everything consists in this, seeing or not seeing the Madonna." He cast a sudden circular glance at his red audience and, finding it still penetrated by what had preceded it, he threatened to call the "Shrink." A sort of wing of youth came out of it, which permeated the old men, ventilated by the likelihood of that threat, as if it were a migraine, and who were now hanging around as in a break from the council, a break destined for coffee. There wasn't any coffee left in the house. They poured themselves drinks, mostly sweet liquors. They were drinking as if it were a celebration. Seated in a circle around his menacing bed, like a collegial visit for an illustrious ailing man. They were bent over, holding their two fingers of rose liquor delicately between their two fingers, like live butterflies. "Seeing or not seeing the Madonna," the ailing man said again, "that's the theme." He entertained them for a long time with the story of Frate Asino; Saint Giuseppe da Copertino, a swine herder, who gave himself wings by frequenting his own ineptitude, and at night, while praying, he reached the altars of the Virgin, flying with his mouth hanging open.

The idiots who see the Madonna have unexpected wings, they even know how to fly and to land on the ground as light as a feather. The idiots who don't see the Madonna don't have wings. They can't fly at all, and yet they fly anyway, and, instead of landing, they fall down again, like some guy with blocks tied around his feet, who wants to untie them, but instead he decides to cut off his feet, dragging himself toward salvation amongst the mockery of the gatekeepers, sensibly confident in the immanent hemorrhage that will stop him in his tracks. But those who see don't see what they see; those who fly are themselves the flight. He who flies is unaware of it. Such a miracle annihilates them: more than seeing the Madonna, they are the Madonna they see. It is ecstasy, this paradoxical absurd identity, that empties the prayer of his subject and in exchange misleads him in self objectivization, within another object. All that is different is God. If you want to embrace someone, you are the intercourse; when you kiss, you are the mouth.

Divine is the illusion. This is a saint. All the saints are like this, fundamentally unprepared, even useless. The altars move toward them, puppeteered by the feeble-mindedness of their own psychoses or by stabilizing terrestrial forces — but this is excluded —. It is in this way that a saint loses himself, through his uncontrolled idiocy. An altar begins there where measure ends. To be saints means letting go, renouncing the weight, and the weight means organizing one's own dimensions. Where a witch has passed, a fairy will pass. If they were to give Frate Asino an apple, half green and half red, half of it poisoned, he, who had butterfingers, would've dropped it by mistake. He could neither lose himself nor save himself, because he was unintentionally inept. He who has never thought about death is probably immortal. This is how one sees the Madonna.

But the idiots who see the Madonna don't really see her, like two eyes staring at two eyes through a wall: transparency is the miracle. Madness is the sacrament, because blind faith closed these eyes; it transformed the strata — the strata were made of rock — it transformed them into veils. And the eyes saw sight. Either man is blind in this way, or God is objective. The idiots who see, see themselves in a vision, with the variations that faith brings: if worms, then they see themselves as butterflies, if puddles clouds, if a sea a sky. And they fall to their knees before this alter ego, as if before God. They confess to a second sin.

Divine is everything that they learned unconsciously about themselves. They saw the Madonna. Saints.

The idiots who haven't see the Madonna are horrified of themselves, they look elsewhere, in their neighbors, in women — in quotidian courtesies turned prayers — and this leads to a myriad of altars. Enthusiasts of communication, they don't bring God to others to access themselves, but rather bring themselves to others to access God. Humility is *conditio prima*. Our contemporaries are stupid, but prostrating ourselves at the feet of the stupidest among them signifies praying. That's how we pray these days. Like always. Spending time with the most talented doesn't mean getting close to the absolute anyway. To be even nicer than the nicest. To finally be the greatest idiot. Religion is an ancient word. These days, we call it education.

He wasn't a saint. The bishops were speechless. The narrator took a break, also because the rain outside had become torrential; it wouldn't allow him to continue in a whisper and be heard at the same time. And the splattering of water, alongside the deafness of the priests, who were all very advanced in age, these were certainly not the best conditions for his speech.

The narrator froze, as did everything else, including the audience. A truly long pause followed, but everyone at attention. They were listening to the rain, until it stopped, and they listened to nothing. They breathed in the odor of the wet dust. Aurora with her rosy fingers blew on the candles without extinguishing them, melting milk and sugar into a lot of Titian red, breathing like a fairy on the sleeping incense, giving a pink hue to the silver and gold in the heart of the treasure room, and his firefly-shaped jewels paled to mother of pearl at her pink breath scented with fresh air.

He, too, was very pale, as he looked out beyond the distant sea, where another treasure was reemerging from the depths of the violet waters in a lot of, ever more, golden scales, violet and gold glistened on another altar.

And up there in the cyclamen sky, he found a half moon, yellow, as if raised from the bow of the boats returning from fishing.

It was undoubtedly the Turkish fleet, whose flag was easily identifiable; that moon was the emblem of Mohammed. "Here we go again," he said, sorrowfully. "Here we go again."

He woke up. White sails in an azure field. If he saw a sail, he'd pour himself a Pernod. He was meditating on the silver creases in the blue water, proffering, "it's a question of fate." While putting down his empty glass, he ran into himself drowsy in the mirror, unable to stop himself from threatening: "You know what I'll do?" After which, he'd have faith in the pause that would follow, guaranteed by the level of panic that he found sufficient; his faith was blind, up to the point of getting a move on and preparing coffee.

While the water was boiling, he'd laugh like a madman, as if titillated beyond measure, imagining little girls who were intent on guessing his plan. "You know what I'll do?" It was an anathema. Anything other than a proposal. But those girls would try to guess anyway. That's why he'd feel overly tickled by their attempts, such as "let's go on a boat ride," or "don't tell me we're going swimming," or "I bet that he'll go back to bed?!" The fact that those girls weren't able to guess correctly gave him a certain energy as well as multiplying his euphoria. He even started washing the dishes, still laughing in an increasingly disturbing manner and responding "no, no, no," one more amusing than the next, to the candor of those suppositions. He moved on to scrubbing the silverware, mostly teaspoons, &

every time he picked up a pan he'd decree "It would be easy" or "That would be great," or in a fatherly fashion "she's so great!" or in a more malevolent manner "if only!" Those girls were pestering him, and he was like a fish in water, more than the plates in the sink were. Now, it seemed as though he had been tarantismized — ah, innocence! — To avoid an eruption of that tarantism, he went out on the loggia, taking off his apron so he wouldn't attract the neighbors' attention. The palm trees, infested with birds, mostly sparrows, shrieked until they convinced him that it wasn't his house, that it was a nursery school playground: useless to understand or contest when it's time for recess. It was better to die of laughter in the kitchen. Taking advantage of the tears he had wept in the previous scene, improvising the tone, never before felt so much, of a superintendent, he ran to the parapet above the roses announcing: "Today is National Tree Day." He was hoping they'd all stand in a line, at least for the speech. Instead, even the cats from below joined in to dig deep holes, to bury and resuscitate themselves among the zucchini flowers in the adjacent garden. "It's crazy," he said in conclusion.

Even better, perhaps more useful, & indisputably more fitting, he'd be a congressman on the other balcony, the one overlooking the sea, negotiating with the Turkish ambassador. Rather than subjecting himself to all these concerns, it was better for him to pretend to be afraid. It was actually a stroke of luck that he had gotten up early. If their intentions were to do again to Otranto what they had done 500 years ago, then they were sorely mistaken. In fact, it was useless to negotiate; at any rate, he didn't speak Turkish. And even if he did? Why come to a compromise? If even a fifth of the damages suffered at the time were true, why try to repair a situation that today was under control? It was clear. He'd have to call Rome. Who knows if he would find her at home. It couldn't hurt to try. Had he always taken advantage of trifles to let the opportunity of a state of emergency escape him this morning? He'd have to call. He'd have sent an interpreter to the balcony. He went there himself, his eyes half-closed in fear of the horde, & asked him, briefly in French, to wait.

In Rome. He'd have forwarded an urgent request. He thought about her. He saw her: unaware of how much was true because this time it was true. This time, perhaps, she'd have seen the wolf. And like a fairy-tale, she wouldn't have believed it. But this wasn't what mattered. What mattered was seeing the wolf, a wolf that wasn't also the dog. Her leaving, he never really knew how to tell that story. In the past, she'd often come to see him. And he had shown her the wolf. Her mouth had tormented him, constantly reassuring him that it was a dog, because it wagged its tail, because if it had been a wolf, it would've eaten her. She would explain everything in a caress and then she would

leave, each time definitively. Thus, for him, the Turkish army, in her hands, would become a wretched fleet
of fishing light attractors struggling in a mundane
sea. If he were to miss this opportunity as well, how
could he ever be afraid again; what would the future
hold? Then again, he could lose her once more, having
already lost her before.

A siege was starting, another one. The town, all in
white, was doing its best to confront it. The odor of
whitewash was everywhere. He was following the
work of the construction workers, the restorers, and
the house painters, all of them mobilized by a prema-
ture summer. This siege would last longer than the
last one. There was a reason for it: the public health
office had, in no uncertain terms, communicated that
the town would not surrender until the last cellar had
been painted and made presentable. Hence the snow
of whitewash, indifferent to terraces and oleanders
alike, & the odor of paint that the dusty wind would
inhale on hotel window fixtures. All of it, from the
top & quickly. But, even if everything had been dili-
gently renovated, that siege wouldn't, in any event, be
over until the insecticide campaign, which had been
promised by city hall, had been carried out. The towns-
people were, nevertheless, tired and weary; even if
they still weren't ready, they'd have willingly opened
the gates to the town and let the infidels in, except
that, fearful of the public authorities, they resigned

themselves to continuing the works ordered by the independent tourist office, wishing for their capitulation, covering up the loggias and balconies with immaculate linens, invoking, without winds and all in tears, the surrender.

He looked out over the balcony on the sea and watched the Turks as they slept within the emeralds, waiting, immersed in their cradles of a new and unexpected patience, disloyal even to themselves, disengaged, exempted from that duty of vintage cruelty of theirs, waiting while avoiding the rubies of the massacre.

There was a Moorish villa next to his house, revealed by the salty sea, Oriental, like a faded reflection, flaking under the vaults of the arches & on the domes. It was inhabited in winter by accommodating Christians, who during the pagan summer would surrender the villa's two seaside wings so they would not die of hunger. Having proclaimed the end of the siege, the villa would've become the general headquarters of the Turks, who, in the violet sun-drenched sky, had furled the half-moons.

On this side of the hot windows, fogged up from the weather, that of his breath, his forehead, his nose, his lips pressed as if a mosaic on the crystals, he'd follow the seagulls coming close to the dilettantism of the merlons and the spires. That piece of architecture was a summary of a story, or not. It was his executioner, converted, precisely when it was his turn, 500 years ago. The executions of the 800 plus martyrs had taken place in a wheat field, and those turbaned colonists had reaped the golden spikes enameled in cinnabar, driven mad by the lure of that mine of faith.

He thought it'd be easy for them to meet one last time on that occasion. Given that it was a saint who was entreating her. So, he had written to her: "come, this time it's serious," and she replied: "don't worry, I really can't come right now, you'll see, everything will be fine." He laid his head on a stone and dreamt of her. He awoke to find that they hadn't yet decapitated him. He looked up, trying to find his executioner & found him crucified. They explained to him that his executioner had been punished in this manner for suddenly changing his faith. Then they told him to get up and get out of there. He hadn't dared make a fuss, though they had humiliated him, no doubt about it, but he'd see her again.

His forehead pressed against the glass, moist with sweat, he was executing himself in a Turkish bath, imagining that it had all gone differently.

If the Moorish villa were true, then it would also be true that today his bones would be on the red velvet in the crypt of Otranto's cathedral, enshrined in the prodigy that would have them still covered in flesh after all that time, like in that other miracle of his, that is, that he was, after all, still thinking about her.

He remained there, motionless, as if in the lost urn, but, unlike the other martyrs, besides the pieces of liver, the membranes, the tendons, he'd saved the eyes, such that the others would see him in an urn, whereas he'd see them in another urn.

That afternoon was one when there weren't many visitors, so few in fact that they had decided to close the crypt and perhaps reopen it in the evening, when the number of pilgrims would undoubtedly have grown.

Outside, on the balcony, at the base of the urn, the white and red lilies had withered. He was saddened by the clerics' negligence.

He would've liked to put a mirror outside, on the windowsill. But what did that bishop think he knew about his vanity? Good God! They were praising his humility, whereas in town they were probably proudly rejoicing in not knowing anything about him.

In any event, he'd remain like that, immobile, his face deformed from the pressure against the glass, disfigured by the sun. He could even do without a mirror on the windowsill. "I see myself seen," he'd think.

At this point, his face was dripping inside a confusion of pearls and diamonds, diurnal stars that, trembling, would fall, extinguishing themselves, and then rise back up ignited by tears, impartial and holy, to assail him with assorted jewels, until his face was lost, a secret treasure within him. Anyone admiring him from the outside would only have seen him crying, also because they wouldn't have ventured to pry open the urn's woodwork and rummage around inside; they would've damned their hands in impossible caresses, and would never have found two black pearls. She was right in calming him down. No one was going to take out his eyes.

He remained immobile, watchful that no one would attempt to take him away. As hard as he tried, he wasn't able to imagine the unholy man who would shatter the urn and embrace him. No one understood his worth. They were marveling at other things on his altar: at his wrecked, but ever abiding, liver, at his cartilage, at the flesh triumphing over its putrefaction, notwithstanding the death that he was living, and, lastly, at the eyes. They even found it normal that he would move around. They venerated him. His success with his worshippers, however, didn't move him at all. A thief would've torn out his heart; that is, if he were either afraid or devoted. It would've been child's play at ten o'clock at night.

He endeavored to tempt himself differently. He shivered under the bronze and the mask of pearls. He controlled himself and began to study; at any rate, the martyrs from the neighboring urns wouldn't have seen him. Perhaps he found a simpler solution and silenced a "now, I'll open the glass pane." No one would've stopped him. Meanwhile, he disapproved of the carelessness with which they left him unprotected day & night. How much could it cost to hire a guard? He'd get out of there. He'd leave on his own. It would've been their loss. He could open the urn's glass pane on his own. He even had a key to the crypt's gate. He'd get out of there. He'd be very careful. Once outside, he'd make his way to visit someone, or maybe to the customs office or the grand hotel; it wouldn't be a problem. He'd be putting them in a difficult situation. They'd arrest them all. He'd have gone to visit them, a mass arrest. Even so, he'd have them catch him with a numerous gang. They'd have found them holding the loot. All their excuses would be useless! For his part, he'd have lit a flame under the furor of whoever was in charge of the search, somehow showing his disdain for the perpetrated offence. He'd perform a miracle. He'd move around, or skip, or close his eyes, perhaps forgiving them; at any rate, they wouldn't forgive them. They'd bring him back in a procession, among a myriad of burning candles to the cathedral; they'd place him in the urn, where they'd station four armed guards in adoration to watch over him in the future.

He was indeed about to leave. The setting sun stained the jewels on his face with blood red, dripping like a freshly-opened pomegranate, illuminated by another sun that was setting on its own.

At first light, he told himself that they had lit the lamps at his feet. It was unlikely that there would be any visitors at that time.

He mechanically tested the doorjamb with one of his fingers. It was the side with the hinges. He was about to raise his left hand, when he heard footsteps approaching the mosaic in the nave. His fears were confirmed when he also heard a screech coming from the little gate to the crypt. And then it opened. The cleric guide moved aside to let someone in. It was her, with no way out. She had entered. She went religiously to the center *&* turned around fearfully on herself. The cleric illuminated the urns. His eyes got lost among the ossuaries. He heard subdued voices, as much as his glass pane would permit him. A guide who was explaining the history of those relics to a woman... "It's important to consider that Otranto's population at that time was 30,000 inhabitants; that was a lot back then. The Turks' landing was unexpected. The city was literally destroyed in a sea of blood after a long siege. There were two types of martyrs, those who fell while protecting the city's walls, martyrs for their country, and those numbering 800, the survivors who, faced with the choice of disavowing their faith in Christ and accepting Mohammad, had refused and were led to a wheat field — you see; that's why golden spikes are present among the membranes and the bones — they were executed, decapitated, or impaled, and are martyrs of the faith. We only watch over the remains of 360 martyrs in this crypt, because the other bodies were taken to Naples by Ferdinando of Aragon. You can still see the flesh, the fingers. This one here has even saved the eyes!"

She closed her eyes and felt faint. The guide asked if she was feeling ill. She told him no, she was all right; she hoped she might just stay a little while by herself, only a little while, to pray. Was that possible? The cleric consented and withdrew.

He was staring at her now, on her knees at the foot of his altar. They said very little, only those things that their amazement allowed. Atonic articulations, what is more, distorted by the glass pane.

"Look at me," he said, smiling at her the same pearls that had fallen from his eyes. "You came back!"

"You always cry..." she said, smiling at him disarmed and "now I want to" she said, lowering her eyes, "now I want to!"

He opened the urn gently and put one foot on the balcony. A swell of tears embraced him as never before. He doubled over, with his lips glued to the balustrade, repeatedly kissing a stone.

He was about to let himself fall, but then he caught sight of someone on the street who turned, alarmedly, in his direction. So, he picked a wisteria.

There were letters that he sent and letters that he didn't send. He decided to stick to the available materials and somehow piece together a narrative, unpublished, and even obscure, as in fragments like: "you're losing, in me, a daughter for your vice-ridden bed, nothing more, created by nature and as sweet as zucchini flowers. A horse is a horse. You're done with all that, right mommy?"

He tried but couldn't remember. It hadn't been excluded from his memory: five centuries ago, during the Turkish occupation, he himself was trying to collaborate with the Tourist office on the staging of a holy performance, which he would direct. The public authorities, who were understandably distracted and had enough on their plates with burying the dead — at that time, Otranto hadn't been conquered yet —, had made it clear to him that such an event would not only be absurd, but it would also be impossible to consequently divert the funds that had been officially earmarked for that mournful event. There was little to play with. They'd have to bury what was possible to bury. If he were intent on insisting, he could preach the impossible to Venice, which, among other things, hesitated to intervene.

"Do we want to do it for the seats?" the city assessor asked him. So, there in front of a wall, he'd explained the commercial possibilities of his production.

Because the city was left undefended, it would've been madness to respond to the Turk's siege, and to delude himself into thinking that it was possible to organize the production. In his opinion, they'd have to elicit as best they could a certain æsthetic style, no matter which one, in each individual, by reciting with disengaged rage and for an audience of convicts any old parable without principles; a parable that would exalt doubt and cowardice, if necessary, and that would suggest an ultimate self-respect, the exception as the only collective possibility, a spiritual prepared-ness for the surrender; that is, if they didn't want to make martyrs out of them. Let the public authorities consider the matter more carefully, before refusing a collaboration that would be decisive for his theater. Let them read up on it. If they were to decide not to sub-sidize him, based on a misinterpretation of the docu-mentation, littered with bad reviews, of his previous performances, their error would've been irreparable. Contemplating at their leisure, they'd have discovered just how much he'd endangered the peace, how he'd attempted a jovial, Carthusian way of operating, by disquieting the sweetness of it, the private and Pom-peian character of sleep. Let them reflect on his hon-esty. Let them conclude: "This man hasn't concealed his failures of which we were, nevertheless, unaware, having been occupied for some time now with the city. This man has shown us his inadequacy in order to encourage us to intervene. Our ministry is helpless. It's no longer a question of organizing the performance. We'll play the Turks' game. We've read the script, absolutely apolitical, wishy-washy, uncritical, a text that we'll censor later, if we're still alive, once we ward off the massacre. These days, it's obligatory to promote unconsciousness. This actor boasts about how bad an actor he is. He even goes so far as to declare himself an idiot. He promises to be able to bring back collective Christianity to personal irresponsibility. What will become of Otranto? Exactly. Who will defend the walls? No one, that's who! Can you imagine the Turks breaking down an open door? They'll come in. They won't find a faith to castigate. They'll be reduced to roaming around the streets of the old town, tourists looking for all the things they should've done, in the evening lost between the inaccuracies of their history, until, scandalized by the prices, they would leave, violating the terms of their cruise contract. A summer season like any other."

Evidently, the town meeting hadn't concluded like that. The person in charge of cultural tourism admitted to him that the council's decision had been indisputably influenced by higher motives, such as the Vatican's concerns regarding the fact that the Church of

Rome would've risked a fall in some stocks in Turkey, if the events in Otranto that year weren't able to bring about a certain result. He should've been able to figure that out on his own, since they weren't intervening. Was he sure? Or, was he intent on moving forward with that subversive performance of his, whatever the cost, to recover one lost sheep and lose the other 99? He responded to the guy from tourism that none of the sheep would be lost, that he could save all 100 of them. If the Turkish army were to move to the North, then he'd take his performance on tour. It was a problem of collaboration. The local bishop was willing to save the whole flock, at least the one in Otranto, and notwithstanding, faced with the immorality of the text, declared that he would rather go to Naples. Once there, he would do everything he could.

Headstrong, he had reread the script. It was an allohistory in which the consequences of faith were imagined and described in a perverse and repugnant manner, but prophetic. Stage directions like headstones, without altering anything from the events to come. They didn't want to give him an audience. They even went so far as to ignore him. Again.

Today, everything had gone differently. In another town. Having finally received authorization from the public health office, this community had ended the siege, with a considerable increase on the tourist tax. They'd have to recuperate from a month of closed doors, consecrated to the renovation of the private residences and to the modernization of the hotels. A white strip impressed by the artifice of the oleanders, perfumed with the scent of Turkish tobacco, indescribable for all the purchases along the street feathered by the colorful footsteps hurrying to the sea.

The Moorish villa became the Turk's general headquarters made pale by its own programmatic quality, or by the sun, in the morning, rethinking the gold and the blood, or oblivious, between the cracks in the plaster, pink and sky blue would bleed out in a silvery sea, like a painted cloud within another cloud of pollen fuming among the arches with withered flowers, stationary in an elsewhere of the serene sky.

There were letters that he didn't send. Urgent requests that really didn't merit the humiliation of a response, words proffered in prayer that the ungratefulness of a final remedy would've annihilated. In those unpublished writings, there should've been a need so simple to satisfy, and therefore unimportant, a need never reciprocated, not even by the love of his love, that had re-opened him to two thoughts or, if you like, re-closed again in a single force, saying "either I come without my letter, or I stay here with it."

He'd have to reread those letters, safeguarded in the bottom drawer to the left of the glass pane of his urn, perfumed by the white solutions she'd imagined.

He'd have to wait until one night, and one night in particular. It would've been impossible to enter the house through the front door, brazenly cross the hall, and reach his room naturally. It would've been impossible to turn on the light and leaf through the letters. Rereading those documents would've amounted to robbing himself. He'd have to surprise himself, perhaps when he was absent. He'd have to absent himself, act as if he were out of his mind, open up a passage through the wall, a hole the size of his body that would lead him to the room of secrets, masked, on the one hand afraid of being recognized and to prevent the tuff from blinding him, and on the other hand to avoid betraying himself at the first mirror. He'd have undoubtedly deafened the neighbors, by chipping away at the wall with a pickax — at that point, there wasn't any other way — and he'd attract the attention of the Turks wandering the streets until late at night, or on patrol in the neighboring garden, or on guard among the Moorish villa's merlons. Perhaps, in the end, he should've prepared another way of getting into the house. He thought not, since the one he had planned was the most honest, because it was the least tempting to share, the most uncomfortable, the one that, more than any other, would express his disappointment and best translate his embarrassment. It goes without saying that he wouldn't have been able to perform it every night, at least not without first finding himself another house, but one night, one night was possible, when, for example, the scandal created by the noise could be mistaken for and even praised as part of a firework display. The San Lorenzo Festival, which the town celebrated in an explosive jubilation of unlimited fireworks, was coming up; he'd have to wait until August 10th. That meant he had a week to get to work on readying the house, to nail up the doors and windows, should he have to leave to allow what he should've prevented. He imagined they had told him that. To prevent is to leave. Going toward oneself, even despite oneself. He dragged a whole box of tools in from the shed *&* got to work. It was exhausting, but he kept at it, except for two hours in the afternoon, during which he didn't even really stop, but rather spent on the more tacit implementations, such as taking measurements, doing calculations, adding everything up on paper, checking on all sorts of things, to avoid getting yelled at by the Turks, who, on the first day, had intimated, from the Moorish bastions, that he shouldn't start pounding before five o'clock in the evening.

He'd have to leave, it's true, but he'd take his time. It wouldn't be any easier for him to come back.

He wound several rolls of barbed wire all along the balcony's balustrade. He assailed the windows *&* the interior doors with crisscrossed boards. He even went so far as to wall up the front door. He hadn't had much experience with masonry, and so it cost him a whole day.

He'd need to finish the renovations the day before the specified date. He shored up everything with huge wooden beams that he secured to the floor with reinforced concrete, and to the shutters, large slabs of quick-drying plaster. Unsatisfied, he decided to wall up the windows as well. When working on the exterior windowsills, he'd proceed very carefully, placing one brick at a time, but gently, because either the Turks or passersby in the area could hear him, or even worse, see him. He preferred to do all the masonry work on the exterior at night. In this way, from one of the last windows overlooking the sea that had been effaced except for one last brick, up there, high above, a moonbeam was filtering in, just one beam, a strand of hair, like a tempting thread from her. He found himself at that moment sitting on a wobbly stool on top of a table, his eyes immersed inside that single wound, weary, out of breath, he heard a woman's laugh sing out. He looked outside, within the limits of the frame intended for him, disconcerted by the laughs that were pursuing one another under the wings of the Moorish arches and, slipping in the echo, were falling onto the dusty oleanders, like him, the whitewash making him a dusty old man, his hands hurting, punctured by splinters of wood, his fingers covered in scratches from the nails or struck due to accidents with the hammer, his whole face covered in plaster, a Lazarus who played at dying and at rising again each day, so that he wouldn't die *&* rise again once and for all. But it seemed to him that a woman up above, far below the moon, from the balustrade's nocturnal east, up above, among the vanished dreams of frescoes, a woman was staring at him. It was unlikely, no one could've seen him. But there he was staring, perhaps at a woman on the balcony of another planet. The oleanders, the spires, and the arches began to quiver, but inside his tears. He felt himself slipping away, like he was about to fall apart, inexpressible, like a monument with an ailing heart. He tried to call out. To whomever might be up above. His eyes closed, but his mouth, pressed against by the still-wet cement, told him its flavor. He let himself fall, sliding down the wall's frame, until he reached the ground. He observed, in astonishment, the hieroglyphics that traced his body as it fell. He wanted to make sense of them, by annotating on the cement with his finger until he fell asleep.

As soon as he woke up, three hours later, unable to think straight, and in a cold sweat at the thought of finding himself in a grave. The plaster, which had dried on his face by then, tightened his features.

He lightly touched the mummified skin with his fingers and wore himself out from grimacing so much while trying to get his lips to move. He'd slept with his mouth open. He got back up on the table and wedged in the last brick and then got down again. To liberate himself from that mask, he even resorted to using a putty knife. He started to peel it off. Then he washed his face several times. His skin remained irritated, as if it had been burned. He scolded himself harshly for his carelessness in using that grease paint for a makeup base. He even started to deride himself, while washing his face, insinuating: "you get what you ask for."

He started getting dressed once he was back in his room. During short pauses, he'd try, without making it obvious, to trap himself in attempts at spontaneous gestures: looking at himself in the mirror, leafing through a magazine, rereading one of those letters. He'd smile, but resentful at the absurdity of such candor, and then moved on by forgiving his desire for its youth.

He had no desire to pack his bags, especially because there was no real need, but he did need to go around town with suitcases that were as sizeable and ostentatious as possible so that people would notice him, even if only in passing. Everyone in town would have to believe only one thing: he was leaving. They'd say, "he's leaving, oh well!" Their comments wouldn't matter, "he left!" My God, if they were to have seen him knocking down a wall in his house, they would've undoubtedly called the "Shrink." They'd have put him in a straitjacket. They didn't mess around over there, that might be because they'd never read anything.

Let's not even talk about the hospitals. There was only one mental hospital and nothing more, crazy or not. He shouldn't take the risk.

The suitcases. Okay. After all, he only had to be gone for two or three hours. He'd get to the neighboring town by taxi. It was six kilometers away. So be it! He'd have to walk back on foot. If he were to have someone drive him back, then that would be equivalent to bringing back a witness. It was best to walk. Yeah, but that would mean he'd have to drag along his suitcases with him on the way back. Six kilometers with the suitcases. So, leave them empty. Their only purpose was to attract attention anyway. The victims of his alibi certainly wouldn't have weighed them, no, no doubt about that. But, like usual, the driver would probably not have allowed him to put them in the car. He would've wanted to do it himself. He gave up. He'd have to put some kind of dead weight in that suitcase of his.

Losing patience, he opened a closet, the first one that he happened upon. He rummaged around blindly and pulled out the most unexpected objects: the tri-color flag, two cylinders, a pack of candles, toilet paper, a woman's dress, a crown of roses, one with thorns, a ream of paper stamped for official documents, the phonebook for Nice, all the while laughing like a hyena, or like an unfortunate card player who, after turning over card after disastrous card, pretends to be content with his own ruin. He packed everything into two suitcases. Then he put on his jacket. Predawn, he went out on the balcony, announcing icily, "Let's eat!" in German.

Actually, all he really wanted to do was sleep. A single glance at the bed was enough to dissuade him. It wasn't a bed anymore, but rather a rough work table, covered in dust from tuff and plaster and littered with nails and tools. He had no intention of clearing it off now that he had cleaned himself up and gotten dressed. Moreover, the sun would be coming up soon, and he'd have to get back to work. Did he desire to reread those letters, or not? He did indeed, oh, so very much indeed! But his dread of another day like that disheartened him to such an extent that it was necessary to come up with a labor union's cavil. This was a trick he'd turn to whenever he was feeling truly exhausted; which was often, and needlessly, because, immediately terrified by the idea of the Institution, he'd back down even revealing himself as athletic, declaring himself better rested today than he'd ever been, swearing up and down that he was "in shape," and, to prove it, he'd lift chairs with his feet, jump over the bed like a fish, and breathing in and puffing out, between one push-up and another, he'd promise: "This time, you'll see!"

He suddenly stopped his gymnastics, telling himself that he was convinced, and also because the sun had risen *&* had playmates in the Turks who, being morning people up to the point of foolishness, were stretching their legs on the Moorish villa's terraces before drowning themselves in coffee. Not this morning, though, because the window on the right side was walled up, but, in the last few days, he was convinced that those infidels were spying on him with the sole purpose of copying his ritual. He hadn't been able to avenge himself. It wasn't worth it. It would've even been easy for him by demonstrating some of his jumps off the balcony for them. They would've imitated him from the spires, ten times the height of the second floor. It wasn't worth it. He ran to the kitchen.

He made himself a coffee. He went out on the little loggia, the one in the courtyard that was the most discrete. He wanted to know how much traffic was on the street. He climbed up on the terrace.

Now, he had a clearer view of the invaders, laughing in their teapots, brandishing teaspoons, lifting up silver teacups filled to the brims with black water to the sky. He could hear them defying the sea, immortal in their porcelain armor, glorious among the seagulls' banners. A blinding white cloud rested itself on the mosque's dome as if it were burning, and, harpooned by myriad gestures, it went away, dragging along an ideal of the Orient, or so it seemed to him, "they're leaving," he thought, "it all returns." He went back down following the tapestry of the stairs, "I'm coming down, I'm coming down," deluding himself. He passed by the mailbox. He stopped, bending over as far as necessary to hug a child, all the while repeating to himself, "I'm inside a sock, next to the bed." He bent down to give him a kiss, or for someone to console him. Then he tied one of his shoes and proceeded.

The day of the San Lorenzo Festival had arrived. At five o'clock in the afternoon, he went out via the kitchen door. He turned the key three times in the lock; he wanted to test its resistance by rattling it. It was fragile, no doubt about it. This last precaution was against eventual thieves, real ones. As for him, he wouldn't have been so petty as to go back that way. His trip had another destination. He hadn't left the house in a very long time. The cicadas' chirping distracted him from every further thought. He sighed, hoping that everything was starting off on the right foot. He picked up the suitcases and listened. Nothing but the raspy murmuring of the fig trees in the neighboring gardens, the terracotta pots spread out between clumps of red earth, undoubtedly swollen with fire, the doors, maybe open, beyond the little curtain of bamboo, the seemingly dead cat. He was about to see his town again. He went down the stairs in a heartbeat. As soon as he was in the street, he looked up at his balcony. He thought they were right to worry about him sometimes. He set off in the warm, festive air of that day. The Turks were coming and going between the rows of oleanders, carrying small terracotta pots or fishing poles, or paper cones of fish or loquats, little kids or tennis rackets, for the most part dressed all in white or redeeming in their flotation rings, arm in arm or flanked on the west side by women in flowery summer dresses, every so often a cherub. There were a lot of cherubs, barely a white meter, with wings & with little roses in their curls and holding white lilies with long stems bound with big bows between their fingers. Having turned a corner, he found himself in the small square in front of the church burning like an enormous candle or an incense cake, to see and to believe, uneatable, since all around, on the outside, the guests in white & in jerkins, and the Turks, under the fake canopies of the archway decorated in red Chinese silk sailing tomorrow, were cracking nuts, devoutly offering little clouds of cotton candy to the cherubs. If one of the cherubs were to get their dress dirty, or fall down, they would be punished with a spanking by a woman dressed in black. A white, red, and green flag had been raised on the balcony to adorn the entirety of the town hall's façade; windowsills, iron grating, parapets camouflaged in a rainbow of banners, the road scattered with rose petals. And the band would be playing something else. Suspended by invisible wires stretched out between the oleanders, rose ornaments, & the as of yet immobile fireworks' whirligigs, hung those skeletons that, when it was dark, would be covered in lights in the manner of incandescent wheels and which would shatter the Milky Way. Thus, up in the air, he saw his master plan fall into place.

Now, he'd have to cross the square and go to the dive bar opposite, between the bazaar and the police station. The idea of having to cut through those throngs of people, while carrying two suitcases, nauseated him, like in his theatrical past, when it seemed as though he had gone beyond the limit's edge of his contemptuous funambulism on this side of the proscenium and would be compelled to go down to the orchestra among an indignant audience.

"He's leaving today, really, the day of the festival!" That's what they'd think. As if! He picked up his suitcases and, with gritted teeth, started to cross the square, attempting to harm as many Turks and Christians as possible, moving forward in a straight line, like an automaton, through the mob, without the slightest deviation for courtesy. If an angel were to have fallen down at his feet, he would've walked right over it. Nevertheless, no one insulted him. They'd limit themselves to expressing their displeasure, which only lasted as long as a footstep; and he'd try to beg their pardon beyond what was required, by pointing to his luggage, mumbling, since he was forced to keep his mouth closed due to an onset of nausea, which was, at times, impossible to hold back. He'd breathe through his nose, biting his lip, swallowing what seemed like gushes of boiling blood. He felt a cold sweat trickling down his nose, a sign that he was about to pass out. Just a few more steps and he'd be saved. In front of him, as if an altar, up against the wall between the bazaar and the dive bar, there was a flower stand with flesh-colored dahlias, much larger than sunflowers, misted with cool water, as if another season. More exhausted than a swallow, but sustained by that vision of his, he bumped into a barrel of fish in brine, where, at this point irrational, he found himself puking, as if in the sink at home. All around him was emptiness. The people closest to him had jumped at least a meter away, like grasshoppers. He was alone, his head immersed in the fish, as if spellbound in that barrel's vortex which an old man, undoubtedly the vendor, was attempting to jerk away from him. The florist came to his aid and helped get him on his feet. Green, his face covered in drool and sauce, his eyes red, irritated by the vinegar. One of the suitcases sprung open, and the tri-color flag glided to his feet. A cherub picked it up and gave it to the Turks who were busy resuscitating him. They said that they needed to clean him up first, and then give him something strong. They dragged him almost like a corpse to the dive bar. As for him, corpse-like, he thought it was the end, that they were dragging him to the chopping block. He would've liked to invoke her, but he couldn't remember her name.

Instead, they put him in a chair, at the very front of the dive bar, one step above the festival. They washed his face with a sponge and gave him a lemon to eat. As much as he kept imploring them to leave him alone, they didn't seem to be planning to go away anytime soon. They were contemplating him. He started vomiting again. He was having a difficult time getting them to understand that if they didn't leave, he would die from it. The remedy was for all of them to be somewhere else. Finally, they granted his wish, some of them returning to their occupations, and others to their amusements. At any rate, he wasn't dying. They left him sitting there, with his two suitcases at his feet and a handkerchief soaked with vinegar in his hand. In a dreamy state, he was looking for something in the festival. The next day, they would've interrogated the whole town, the whole town witness to how he was there, with two suitcases, and in fact, how he hadn't been feeling well. Every now and then, they'd ask him, "how are you doing?" and he'd nod his head, or they'd say, "you see? it was nothing," and he'd smile.

He even felt well enough to leave, but he preferred to remain a little while longer on that gibbet, because you just never know.

When possible, he'd kick one of the suitcases, nudging it as much as needed for someone to trip over it. He wasn't alone. He also had luggage. Being ill doesn't mean leaving.

"He was in such a bad way that he decided to go to bed." That couldn't happen. Instead, right then, it so happened that a tall, lanky, and inattentive Turk bumped into the suitcase and tumbled all the way under the bar's counter. The infidel turned around, rubbing his head, in pain. Then he started complaining, explaining in a Lombardian accent how that place was not a luggage storage. He was smiling at so much invaluable immoderation, while slightly cradling his head. The Turk, who was calmer now, lifted the suitcase that had landmined him *&* started picking it up and putting it down here and there, demonstrating the many different spots in that bar that could accommodate the contraption, without putting the entrance in peril. Assuredly, he got up, having regained his strength, and offered a drink to the unfortunate "witness," who accepted.

"Did you know that you have an accent…" he said, as if he'd lost something.

"I was born on Lake Como…"

"Not all that long ago…"

"No, not that long…"

"When?"

"The 27th of January, 1923."

"Great!" as if he had found it.

"Why, do you like it?"

"The lake?"

"No…"

"My name is..." he said his name without saying it. The other guy was clearer. "What a strange homonymy... Would you mind repeating it?..." He wasn't sure he'd heard right. The Turk pronounced his first and last name.

"Ah, I got it!"

"What??..."

"It's not him." But he, on the other hand, thought it was.

"It's not a homonymy." He lifted his shoulder as if that pained him.

"Too bad... I really liked this place," the Turk said.

"Why too bad?" he asked, moaning.

"Because I'm leaving, I'm leaving tonight."

The only witness was leaving. He was about to vomit again, this time on the counter, but he held himself back. The concept of his fellow human being was leaving. It was his alibi that was leaving. Luckily, others had noticed him. But he had dedicated himself to this exchange in particular. All that without even a well-earned legal advantage? He'd smothered his malaise, only in the name of an indifferent exchange of words. Yes, that fellow of his was not a witness. Suppose that the planned irruption were to create problems for him tomorrow, would he be able to use that conversation in any way? "I was with a guy who left town!" Is that what he would've said?

The sun was setting. He said "the check," "have a good trip" and exited.

"Tonight. It's now or never!" he said, ordering the driver of an old Fiat 508, also called a "balilla," but thinking about the destination, which he, instead, kept to himself. Having been asked amiably again, he told the man where to go, keeping "it's now or never!" to himself. The car made its way slowly through the festival on the dirt road, surrounded by rocks and prickly pears. He'd only need to imagine the return trip to feel like he was straddling a hippogriff. Every now and then, he'd quietly mutter "why?" and the driver, believing that he'd been asked a question, told him not to worry, explaining that this was the only road. "Wanna bet they won't stop me?" he thought, as two cops on a motorcycle came toward the car. Sure enough, they continued on their way. No season truly exists in which love renounces vanity. Desire, oh everything is desire! Not so fast, you're right, why before a star falls? You'll see how many of them will fall tonight. You don't have time to want only one thing. Falls. And isn't it precisely at this moment that you begin to express yourself, calling desire this deranged vanity of yours? I loved her. You are what people call "how much time has passed" when two old friends meet again, and, having been mistaken, say it anyway, and having become friends, they tell each other everything, & then they say, "how much time has passed!" We love each other, like when we can't take climbing the stairs anymore, and we go for a swim. Everything blended together, like when the second act begins but none of the lights had been turned on. To betray is to conjecture about ancient Egypt. Once we're on the ground, where will we go? Once we're on the ground. In any event, let's descend, there's nothing on earth as sweet as you are. Let's sleep now. "Ah, to see her again!" or "That coward, lying to me up to this very day!" oh you yourself or her what about her, come here oh where are you! In effect, with her it wasn't the month of May. Oh, like the peaches or like the loquats and the apricots, the prunes, and the black cherries, the moscato grapes and the cherries, the watermelons from Brindisi and the carobs, fresh fruit salad, she was crazy about canned pineapples. I am she who has changed her tastes. To see her again! It's like saying lost and lost again. Forgive me, it was only for the strangeness. Because it is strange: sometimes, if I offer her a rose, saying "this pansy is for you," and then I say "give me back that pansy," she, confused, gives me back a pansy. To see her again! Mine, only mine is the presumption. Mine this speechless Easter in mid-air. Grace in the name of inexperience.

A true grace every time. Thank you so much because you are not a fairy tale, but all of them together, all my possibilities to make the same mistake again, my dear, without getting you back. Not anything else. This is why it was over for us. He knew every one of her letters by heart. The driver had asked him a while back where he wanted to be dropped off. Receiving no response, he decided to stop the car in the middle of the town square.

It was evening. "Turn around, for goodness sake!" the half-sleeping client implored him, "it's too far from here. Drop me off at the town limit. There's a bar there. There would be great." They turned around. He got out at the last white & pink houses. That watering hole was closed. The locals had undoubtedly poured into the neighboring town, at sunset, to enjoy the fireworks display. "All the better," he thought. Here, he really didn't need a fellow human being. On the contrary, the fewer the better. So, he didn't get a coffee. "From the top," he said to himself. Without a full stop, from the top with two suitcases. Luggage in hand, he headed toward a row of elm trees. When you are the wait, the voyage is strenuous, "who knows what she's doing right now" or "she really isn't waiting for me" or even "she'll turn pale." You won't be able to surprise her with anyone anymore, or wake her up. This voyage is you without adventure. You know the others are all liars. What can they do there, if it's enough? When you translate "enough" as "no more." But it's not enough for you. I want to make myself an unexpected event. I lived. An outcome is not a destiny.

You don't see me and I walk and this approaching does not exist, she will embrace me. So many elm trees! It's a row. There were soon olive trees, verdant ossuaries to the luminary, black at the extremities of nightfall. Then you said to me: "My little girl is not a baby doll, she is the little girl of my baby doll of a little girl. I told a lie and it came true. They sleep in the same bed, my little girl in the same bed with my baby doll, like a sole sole solitary mommy simply sole, sole like a mommy without a mommy. I told a lie and it came true. To rock to sleep is to let yourself be rocked to sleep or it's fatigue. All of that is watchfulness, patience, and fatigue of loving, never again, never ever to rock asleep faltering from fatigue."

To rewrite you! See, if only you were to see how I'm distancing myself, in order to surprise myself from afar in good faith. Mommy, why can't I call you mommy? Seeing as how the olive trees never end, my curiosity may pray eternally thus.

If only your voice wouldn't stop! They spoke about anything & everything. To rewrite you. I'm no longer the author. If you'd wanted or had what you thought, or if what you thought you didn't have, the road where I walk; if not even your maternity invented me, then it's true.

It wasn't productive to walk with two suitcases on the side of the road. What if they'd seen him. He'd taken, while meditating, an imaginary path among the olive trees, so very long ago, attentive, asking every so often, "are you tired?" And in veils, from another rosier disquiet, perhaps from the cyclamens scattered in the sky, her voice responding, "and you?"

"Let's do something else. While you get undressed, I'll bury the suitcases," he said, irrational, "we'll get there before the fireworks start." He got to work on digging with both hands. When she was completely naked, he buried her. So much dirt, red but not a promising evening red; & then, addressing her dress resting on a tree branch, crazy in love, he asked her: "Should we get going!"

It was still or it still seemed to him to be following a much lighter dress. But always carrying two suitcases in his hands, struggling, his throat raw from the vomit, braving the clods of scorched dirt, repeating to himself every time that he thought he was going to die "I'll do what I want" or "finally!"

Now he was walking closer to the main road, but further down from the shoulder, and the sound of a bell was coming his way, enveloped in a cloud of dust, "the mountain that's coming to me," and inside the invisible bell someone was singing, invoking lots of women by their names. Obviously, a madman or a shepherd returning from the fields with his flock. Once he got much closer, it turned out to be three carefree little rascals behind a bunch of goats. Those ladies were walking in silence, but their escorts, who were perhaps tired of raving about them, excited at the glory of the firmament's splendor, or from the pangs of hunger, they'd decided to spend the time that separated them from the laid dinner table, by extinguishing the fireflies amassed along the sides of the road with a hailstorm of stones. He, being exhausted and having put down his luggage, had camouflaged himself, without realizing it, right in the middle of an electric bluish bush, hands down the most splendorous one of all. "Look at that guy!" they said, pointing at him, as if he was the handsomest one of all. They couldn't see him clearly, but throw stones at him, yes, that they could do. Those little shepherds applied themselves to extinguishing his altar to the very last candle. At first, he was crouched down like an oyster, trying to worm himself into the ground. He felt the shudders of the stones lacerate him and the wounds blossom, like disorderly flowers, and the stones in his flesh become precious from his blood. They'd bury him tomorrow. When he reopened his eyes, he felt no pain from his wounds, but it would, nevertheless, have been better if he didn't try to move, and instead tried to sleep, to keep his eyes shut as long as they were bleeding. Like when he'd be sleeping beside her, expecting them to find him. He'd never wake up again. He opened his eyelids with his fingers for a single second and then closed them on the Moorish castle not far off in the distance. And he was surprised by it.

Had he already ridden that far? The fireworks had started. He thought that they were still fighting in Jerusalem, that he wouldn't have the fortune to reach the walls. Assassinated in an ambush, he thought the others would have succeeded, while he wasn't given the chance to liberate the holy sepulcher of her who was his heart. At least not to him. He wanted to pray: "... this voyage suits you, as if, when at night, the sea seems to be no longer there, that there is no longer the sea, as if a night at the sea appears, this voyage suits you, because you don't know how to walk... *Benedictus fructus ventris tui, Dolorosa,* placed and placed again *in mulieribus,* oh, sit down, oh falling. To see is to fall... You are of the morning for playing with dolls that at night transformed into a little boy the next day. The lap is the landscape in which you were conceived by a blessed painter, at the window not yet painted, contemplating perhaps stones perhaps rivers, planned, because you are first, contemplating, you are holding up a child on the parapet, he, too, is watching the drawing of the land where he would be born... Sorrowful is he who observes you in prayer, cradling this going and coming from the future. They'd drawn us in the end. But first the flower *&* then its season, a violet but before a violet, there was first a love before love ended naturally... Amen."

Here Saint Margherita reappeared to him, illuminated in the artificial reflections, perched atop a fig tree. She was saying to him excitedly, "Come up here, come up here! How is it possible that you never like anything? You can't see from down there, come up here if you want to enjoy the fireworks properly!"

Tomorrow, they would come to collect the dead and the wounded. Now it seemed that the sky was exploding. The Saint, in the tree, was flirting enraptured, eating figs and provoking him with the peels, until he started to cry. Soon that crossed assault in the nocturnal sky would die down, postponed until the following year. Even if he survived, so much respite would've made him insane. He had to reach the walls at all cost, even on hands & knees if he had to. He had to find those documents. He got up on his feet and, while dreaming, having picked up the two suitcases, he got back on the road. At that moment, the clumps of dirt would've been impractical.

If he were to fall down again, he wouldn't be able to get up a second time. About a kilometer separated him from his treasure. He went so far as to run, terrorized by the dust that, raised in this way, was in contact with his injuries, threatening him with a decisive infection. Another reason to hurry. Once he got home, he'd disinfect his wounds, take some medicine, save himself in every sense of the word, bandage himself, cover himself in unguents, and smear himself with magical herbs. Once he got home, he'd have all the time in the world to read.

The Saint, seeing him go away, had first challenged him: "I don't know if I'll be here when you get back!" Then she started to cry, yelling after him that he was an ingrate, an egomaniac &, finally suffocating herself in an attack of hysteria, she'd insulted him, threatening that he'd hear soon "about those things" concerning her that he undoubtedly wouldn't like.

As for him, he was desperately running. If he were to encounter someone, he'd throw himself into a ditch. The ground, boomed by the blasts, was threatening to crack itself open. It seemed to him that he was running on a drum. If the magnesium sky, scratched by a deafening crackle, was losing flowers and fringes, it was evident that the Turks' garrison between the Moorish villa's domes was doing everything all wrong. Much ado not about nothing, provided that it lasted as long as his undertaking required. At the entrance to the town, he told himself that it would be best to decenter himself and proceeded along a small road. He would've liked to check his wounds without stopping, but, not having his hands at his disposal, they being anchored to the suitcases, he gave up. He made his way through other people's gardens. Climbing over the walls: first, he'd throw the luggage over the obstacle; then he'd climb up to the parapet and let himself fall, on the other side, with all the weight of a dead body. Fortunately, they weren't all rose gardens, except one, but that was enough to disfigure his face.

Only one garden now separated him from his place. The wall here was higher; nevertheless, he'd have to tackle it in a flash, because the penultimate wall that he'd hurdled with incertitude had catapulted him onto the street. No one. Although he heard voices coming closer from the nearby cross street. And, in addition, the headlights. He stopped in his tracks, terrified. Where did that other suitcase go? There weren't any bushes. And to add to his devastation, the fireworks had ended. Was it possible? Were they really done? Or perhaps it was an intermission, but a fatal one. He could hear bits of conversations, euphoric, undoubtedly the Turks, and footsteps from a throng of people about to turn the corner, right beneath that street light. He began turning himself round and round like a moth, until, utterly wild with rage, he shook the hell out of an oleander. The missing suitcase fell heavily on his head, as if from the sky; it had remained, in the preceding flight, tangled up in the foliage. Another firework exploded like a bomb, shattering, up on high, myriad tiny purple mirrors. The complicity of this last unexpected intervention provided him cover for both his agitation and his screams of pain, which were uncontrollable at this point. He threw both suitcases in the direction of his courtyard, well beyond the wall, and followed them, scurrying like a hunting dog hot on the heels of his falling prey. Barking, irrational, he tried with a jump to touch the edge of that fortification. His grip wasn't enough and he fell again, scraping the tuff, destroying his nails, supine, against the shattered glass of the golden sky. He got up again, and, howling, confronted the wall again. This time with a better outcome. He remained up there, hugging the stones, as if he were just another stone among them. The Turks passed him below and vanished. He studied how to avoid letting himself fall like a corpse. He lowered himself by using the full length of his arms; he let himself fall to the ground clumsily, hurting his throat on an abandoned scythe. A serious gash. He brought his hand up as if to caress himself and felt it completely soaked. He wanted to look at it in a light of amethyst and was shaken from an onset of panic concerning a hemorrhage. He took off his raincoat, ripped his shirt in two large strips, and bandaged himself with them. Once he was home, he'd find a remedy for that too. He put his raincoat back on, closing it at his throat. He found his suitcases and thought back on that scythe: it was truly strange that it found itself there, among the squash, and all rusted to boot. Him, he locked all his tools in the woodshed; and, furthermore, he didn't remember ever having one like that. He climbed the stairs, exhausted, and even the stairs seemed strange to him. And the palm trees, there had been two of them. Where did the other one go?

He noticed these variations more by touch or by smell than by sight. The eyes, it was a miracle that he had saved the eyes. He stumbled over a pickax: he remembered having put this, too, in the woodshed the day before his Crusade. He put down his luggage and approached the kitchen door.

It was open. How did they get it open without damaging it? He was about to go in, but he was ashamed of himself. The last firework was cracking the night sky, and that night was the only possible night. Actually, there wasn't a moment to lose.

He went to the wall, in his opinion his room's wall, and, getting a better hold on the pickax, hit it repeatedly from the force of the hardships of his voyage. Regardless of the outcome of that battle, every knight on both sides of the battlefield would either die or live unhappily, and, tomorrow all the others would've lost everything or found nothing. The dream that was up for grabs was worth the certitude of that tenson of his, and for no other. Cudgel and hatchet, he was pummeling a resistant shield, made of stone, that's true, but with the fragility of a wall. They were infatuated with an elsewhere of blood that the fresh air would've forgotten by dawn. In his heraldry, there was a tangle of gestures that, once executed, would've returned to his mistress a handkerchief dedicated to her, at the time of a tournament that was planned but never took place. There was a tomb for which he had a key that he lost, while walking away in doubt, only to return believing in conquering it. Or it was her, she was at the bottom of the sea, drowned, and he, immersed, who was risking his life by attempting to recover her rings.

These were magical walls. That neglected knight was continuously striking his unyielding adversary in the same spot, even though defenseless. It had been written by him that this home would become a treasure trove. Gold in his heart. Outside, rocks instead of tuff. He was already covered in white under the falling plaster, when the dragon, unforeseeably, suddenly crumpled to the floor. He had just enough time to get out of the way, and wearily reach the stairs' balustrade. A breach opened itself up from the upper part of the terrace, provoked, perhaps, from a weak spot in its invulnerability, a debris of dust and of tuff, all the way to the ground, not unworthy of the final salvo, celebrated in the artifice of the melee. A little less uproarious, this one of his, because it was more authentic. A sympathetic victor, he didn't neglect to consider the damages that he himself would undertake to repair, and he entered religiously, moving through the rubble with humility, recognizing in his implacable and happy hand the mark of the author. The slaves could consider themselves pardoned, effective immediately, and were free to leave, since the economy of his solitude was unable to contemplate servants. What on earth was happening? And what did all this mess mean? Was it possible that he had mistakenly gotten the wrong room? Yes, it was possible. He tried to find the light switch. In vain. He lit a match. Strange, very strange knick-knacks! Bunches of things in piles or scattered around. A burglary. Well, he'd predicted it. The walls were pink. That the thieves were able to expertly force the kitchen door, that they were able to ransack the place looking for money, that they were able to walk away with a palm tree, it was conceivable, or at least for him, he was capable of believing it. But that they'd modified the wiring and repainted the walls? Well, that would really be too much, even for him.

It's true, he couldn't see very well, but, as bewildering as the error might've been, he'd have knocked down the entryway's façade. An essential arrangement of objects that he certainly couldn't reconstruct from an entryway he'd never seen before, let alone in the current state of his health. He was not at all calm. Even so, he'd have to finish it, also because he was feeling faint. His battle was done and the day was his. There was no point in informing the others to stop it. He'd be in his room, had he had the good fortune or the presence of mind to open up a breech a meter further. Had he ended up on the balcony among the lilies, it would have been easy for him to fix it. Instead, the God of armies had launched him into the hall, into the room of compromises, where he was usually defying the folly to cross it. The fireworks were coming to an end. Someone, but quickly, needed to intervene, even by coming in through the bathroom door. He'd have to make himself as comfortable as possible. Someone, like him, who cared a great deal about those documents, for love or for making a fortune, someone who might be able to turn them into money. They would've talked to each other briefly. "Come on, stop faking it!" he said, suddenly indignant, to the editor. "Sit wherever you like. Let's not mince words." Then, imagining that the intruder was being evasive: "You can't lose me in preambles. You came here to rummage around, certainly not with ill intentions, don't be offended; you're the expert. You have the instincts. You want to publish those letters. I'd recommend them to you myself, if I dealt with narrative, on your behalf. No need to apologize. I understand why you barged in here. You thought I was dead. If that had been the case, you would've spared me from the newspapers. I should owe you one." Very determined to cut to the chase, he omitted curiosities, such as, "Why did you move the electric wiring?" or "What did you do with the other palm tree?" or, one last one, "Why on earth did you repaint the walls?" "I'm alive. I don't know if it'll sell. The manuscripts are unfinished. It can be done in a month. I'll get them for you from the other room. In the meantime, write me a check, you'll understand, I'll have to dedicate myself. For me, it's a question of tranquility... I know it's not customary to advance money to first-timers... I'm forced to ask it from you, in both mine and in the publishing house's interests." He interrupted himself, convinced that he'd been interrupted by objections, like "You have to understand," or "Let's not forget that every single decision I make is submitted to an administrative committee," "I'd be putting myself on the line," followed by flattery and confessions in the manner of "The fact that I decided to barge in on you is enough to prove to you how committed I am to this," or "Honestly, the fact that I found you alive is very encouraging," or from uncertainties made up of "How can we be sure that you'll finish the book?" and from "Since I was convinced that you'd excuse my somewhat harsh language, I wanted to speak to you frankly."

Even if it had truly existed, he never would've seriously imagined how the literary and commercial outcome of that encounter was contingent upon the duration of a firework. "As a personal favor," the editor said in conclusion, "I'll send you an advance. First, you'll need to sign the contract, and this, too, they'll first have to send it to you."

Coming to his senses, the author said hurriedly: "Wait here!" not because he'd accepted, and he went out from the gutted wall, stumbling on the crumbled tuff. He picked up the pickax, leaning on it, he lifted it up, and dealt a blow only "here," since a meter should've been enough. What followed was an incredible collapse of hollowed out bricks, pieces of plaster, and dust. The entire façade crumpled, part of it in the interior, and the bulk of it on him. He took advantage of it rather than complaining about it. At this point, his body was a numb mush.

On hands and knees, he traversed the ruins, promising not to be surprised if there were an abyss awaiting him. He entered the room that had only three walls by then. He got back up on his feet, leaning on who knows what. Now the fireworks had ended. His heart stopped, just like his anxiety. Somewhere close to him, in the dark, & he couldn't guess where, a child was crying, but more like screaming. Empty, nonexistent, he opened his eyes wide, without, however, passing out or waking up. An autonomous reasoning prevented him from attempting the entirely mechanical movement of turning something on. That crying would die down in intervals of unrestrained sobs, as if scattered in the dark, always in different obscure places. Someone, whoever that might be, but it was a child, in the throes of dismay, was moving around blindly. He heard that someone run into chairs, everywhere, and so the wheeze became an animalistic terrorized scream again. At the mercy of his wonder, he felt someone clutching his legs. He moved his papier-mâché hand, animated by a miracle, and touched, touched a knee covered in sores and, just above it, a child's head; he stroked the child's hair, absent. That little terror clung more tightly to his wounds.

The saint wore a grimace of a painful resurrection on his face. He understood. He detached and lost his fingers in a magic spell, among the locks of hair of such fear, putting to sleep within them his dread of having been seen appearing. A mere disquiet, his other hand unwound from the draperies of the marble, he lifted the child up to the tops of his arms in an imaginary cross. Kissing his prodigy on the forehead, he caught sight of a small lamp at the foot of his altar, a votive lamp he'd never noticed before, a flicker shipwrecked in the oil, soon thereafter a sphere containing the holiest Saints Cosmas and Damian, physicians, in a day lost in snow.

"Footsteps!" He heard, or thought he heard, bare feet, confident, going toward that ruined sanctuary of his, unless it was someone slowly returning home on tiptoe.

"Voices!" He closed his child's mouth, with two fingers, unless it was her voice, who, after all, was asking again, "How do I get through?!"

He wasn't in his house. That room wasn't his room, nor was the room before it his. He'd flung his two suitcases, when in the street and, blind, had imitated their trajectory, discomfited by the Turks' sudden appearance. The high wall was the same wall as his, because it was a shared wall. He'd fallen into the garden next door. He'd seen a palm tree because only one was visible. He'd found the kitchen door open because that's how they'd left it. The walls were pink because they were pink. On the other hand, there he was holding a sleeping child in his arms, without a because. The footsteps, hurrying along, were those of people undoubtedly returning home. In the glow of the votive lamp, he found a cradle and laid down all his innocence there, except for the irresponsible lightness, the tormented chivalry of an errant night. On the threshold that he'd improvised, backed against the arch, dreamt-up by his pickax, he considered the damages of the consequences. He really hadn't been able to tell if that wall he'd demolished had been a load-bearing wall. If so, a catastrophe would've ensued. Truly sorry, he was hoping someone would come home soon. Hidden among the squash, in the safety of a lush fig tree, he'd have waited dutifully for anyone who, after having seen the accident, would pull that child from his mine-strewn sleep. In the meantime, he'd catapulted his luggage into the neighboring garden, this time his own. He couldn't show himself. He stayed there, a zucchini flower in his hand, as if in the depths of his being, very far away, a sentry on duty guarding his folly. Troubled by other things, no. Since the crickets' reproaches, the other people's returning home from an exceptionally late dinner, weren't a penance. Without the comfort of a futile predicament, frequent with men, when they say: "I did it for you!" There'd be an explanation the next day. Others would've repaired a wall. Him, what else should he wreak havoc on? Perhaps hope is this spelling out day by day. He stayed there. Soaked by, oh if only it were, a medicinal moon. He stayed there, like an obstacle, fallen on his feet, waiting the time it takes to turn a page.

Someone was going up the stairs now. He climbed up the wall and let himself fall into his garden. He wouldn't ever read her letters again, at least not this year. Even before treating himself, he'd have to make things right; that is, if he didn't want to end up implicated in that night's bumbling drama of his. How humiliating, to have to break down a set that hadn't been used. And that wasn't the only thing. He'd have to build another one. He'd die from exhaustion long before he could become an idiot. That undoubtedly unstable house bordered his own. He had destroyed it with the same amount of love. He'd forgotten the pickax among the ruins. Besides, that battering ram wasn't his; he'd found it there. When they'd reconstructed the accident, tomorrow, that device wouldn't have added anything useful. The madman had only used it occasionally. Evidently, he hadn't come armed to that undertaking, and, therefore, having been unprepared, he hadn't in any way premeditated the crime. He'd done the right thing in leaving it there in plain sight. More importantly, how would he have justified the walled-up windows in his house? Would they have deduced that there had been two madmen that night, one good and the other bad? Did they divvy up the work between them, each one to his task? Did they decide on, like in every book, two contiguous houses, two locations in which to expiate, in different ways, a third sin, the one tearing down and the other building up? Or was there only one madman, at the mercy of two different vocations? Good God, he was losing time and blood, inopportunely. Everything was actually much simpler. He had to clean up his mess, and make everything like it was before he went on his trip. When he'd walled up the side windows, the ones facing the Muslim arches, he'd proceeded very carefully, on this side of the little bamboo curtains that, having been lowered before the work had begun, would certainly not have permitted the infidels to notice the developments taking place there. He had to unblock those windows, dislodge the wooden beams leaning against the balcony's shutters, unwind the barbed wire from the balustrade that looked out over the sea, unpack the suitcases, return the tools and the ladder to the woodshed, medicate himself, sleep. Only one hitch remained. If they were to show up at his door, to interview him or even interrogate him, how would he have explained his wounds, scratches, and bruises? So, on the previous afternoon, he was meant to go on a trip. As soon as he'd arrived at the town square, he'd felt unwell. But he'd gotten into a taxi anyway. While en route, his condition had worsened. So, he'd returned home. He'd gone to bed. Clearly, the criminals were spying on him while he was leaving, and believed the house to be empty. To tell the truth, at one point, he thought he felt the walls of his room shaking, but the din of the fireworks misled him, giving him no reason to suspect anything was amiss. He didn't remember anything after that. He'd woken up under a pile of rubble. That's all he knew. Let the police sergeant come into his room, if he'd like, and verify that window there. He'd had it walled up a few days or so ago: the Turks' games were distracting him. How the thieves had been able to pinpoint the most imaginary portion of the wall would, according to him, forever remain a mystery. He didn't remember the names of the bricklayers who'd carried out the work; he hadn't asked them. He'd submit a complaint "against unknown suspects." The police sergeant would've sat down *&*, plucking on his type-writer, impatient, would've started singing: "And here present before me...!"

But no, it shouldn't happen. None of this should happen. Those neighbors of his, the victims of his mistake, knowing him to be a companion in misfortune, would've felt justified in paying him a visit, he, too, having been threatened by an inexplicable act. So, what did he intend to do? As for them, they would've reacted. Could they take a look at his room? The damage had been more severe at their place. An entire wall, they'd have to see. Would he come by their place? Was that a promise? He'd have to avoid that. Supposing he couldn't, how on earth would he be able to tear down that perfectly cemented, though artificial, walled-up space once more, and from the inside to boot? That would mean he'd have to pile up the tuff *&* the rubble in his room, on the bed. Therefore, he'd have to do it from the exterior, by working, among other things, at the top of a ladder, under the uninterrupted scrutiny of the Turks. They would've put him in a straitjacket. In any event, he'd have to do it right away. There was, indeed, a way. For example, by working in silence, cutting out a block of tuff at a time with a saw, but, in deliberately uneven blocks, on purpose, and then breaking them up in little pieces with a hammer, after having rolled them up in a bunch of rags. A Carthusian endeavor. Peace of mind.

He'd have it completed by Christmas, just in time to astound his neighbors and the carabinieri with the likeness of that nativity scene of his. He would've become a bowlful of rose petals for Herod's guards, patience embodied, under the breath of wine and of ricotta, of the clumsy shepherds in adoration.

No one saw him return home. He'd stay locked up in the house, a week would've been enough, in his opinion, the time for his wounds to close up. He'd implement more than one precaution. In the first three days, he wouldn't open the door to anyone. Not that he'd be expecting any visitors. But that wouldn't mean anything. Perhaps visits were awaiting him. On the fourth day, he'd open the door only to the grocery delivery boys, as if just returned home, and displaying the bothersome suitcases in front of the door. He'd first apply an undercoat of greasepaint to his face &, as soon as they'd started knocking, he'd run to the bathroom to lather all his possible faces in soap and, finally, holding a shaving brush, he'd open the door, saying, "Put it right there!"

He couldn't turn on the lights. He lit some candles that he put into the closets, so that every room, bathed in semi-darkness, would enjoy the glow safeguarded in the hollow of his ciborium; a lacustrine manner of his, which he'd adopted in the past, like an everyday luxury that provided him at one and the same time both light and dark.

He removed all his clothes and, after having meditated for a moment with his eyes closed, he approached the mirror. He was standing in front of the reddest and most disarming "Deposition" he'd ever seen. His body was homework poorly done, with errors marked in red that an elementary school teacher attributed to distraction, or to hasty copying; marked-up homework that needed to be saved because it was pertinent in a live composition *&* field, still in time. The proof was all that white space available on his beautiful white skin, unless tomorrow his skin would turn blue. For now, no, because the time allowed wasn't enough. Perverted people may say that "it's written," but who cares? What if the angels are the ones who proofread? He was pretending to be lost in contemplation; instead, he was searching among his many wounds for the most grievous one, a permanent scar, smiling at fears, like "definitive," "irreparable," and at temptations, like "you learn something new every day," "everything has its purpose!"

"Deposition" from the cross. Perpetrated not in pity of his arms, which had a femininity about them not in their deceptive, discernable allure, but in their yielding devotion, a calling, an aptitude for the figure, and their mathematic, sweet, and soft certainty to reclaim a heart rent in two, displaying a flesh wound. Yet, not in pity of his arms. He wasn't yet a heap of tattered affections pleading for a break from his ruthless rhythm;

his suffering hadn't yet been gleaned by the love of three women brought together by the centuries. Let them drive away the child, that Giovanni — John the Baptist — from that absurd vigil, or let them not reprimand him for playing with the flowers & the little flames in his burial chamber. Above all, to the scribes: let them not cite, let them write about a separate case. It was more than proofreading, he was looking in an honest crystal, very far from reflecting him. With all those sores, he could've even pretended to be on his deathbed. Even go so far as to preach and then perform the miracle of going away. He looked at himself in the mirror. By then, he was in a public square. They were demanding. He turned toward their gazes. And he didn't dare — couldn't look at himself. He opened the smaller of his suitcases and pulled out a crown of thorns. He'd never attempted to wear it in this manner before. He'd never spoken to them with their best interests at heart. But what did that mean? The fact that he would not descend so low to the baseness of mimicking them, didn't mean he didn't love them. Even tonight, he wouldn't have projected slides.

"I'm not feeling so hot!" that was how he'd wanted to start. He'd discovered that the ear is the heart, and the heart the ear, and that, in any event, the eyes had little to do with anything. That evening he'd have talked about himself, a topic like any other. That evening, his autobiographical slant shouldn't have alarmed them. That evening, he'd have entertained all of them altogether differently, with a great deal more seriousness than usual. Let them not be angry with him before it started. Let them vanish while he was putting on his make-up. He was alone. He'd lowered himself into a hot bath. Having reemerged, he moved closer to an illuminated icon from which he took out some cotton pads, gauze, alcohol, and various types of bandages, as well as an array of unguents. He sprinkled himself with a certain kind of disinfectant powder, & Saint Margherita reappeared to him, saying: "Let me do it, I'll do it!" and she started bandaging him up while supplicating, "Tell me if I'm making it too tight!" "No, no, no!" he said, about to pass out, & the Saint, having misunderstood, continued energetically, while bent over her embroidered garments. He heard an impatient crowd & suggested, "quickly, quickly!" The Saint stood up, close to rage, threatening: "You're staying with me tonight!" He tried to get up. He was so tightly wound up that he couldn't. "Let's listen to a little music, eh?" said the fairy, and, seeing him shake his head in disapproval, added: "Softly, softly ok?" In any event, he didn't have a say in the matter. She approached the gramophone, ethereal. His pupils, between the bandages, were two terrorized pinwheels. "Amado mio!," what madness! Always more beautiful, the Saint, after having torn away & placed in a drawer the beams leaning against the shutters, opened the urn's glass pane on the balcony to the perfumed night. He was groaning. "Come here, I'll take you to see the sea!" Having said this, she lifted him up in her arms, and, kissing every hair on his head, she dragged him outside to the veranda, lovestruck, repeating to him: "Do you think that a mortal woman could love you this much?" He nodded his head, perhaps, insensitive, taking her at her word. He'd wanted to confess that, yes, there was one; one that might love him. If she cared about him, she'd put him to bed. Actually, he hadn't given her permission to open the window, let alone to go out on the balcony, and, even worse, together. If she cared about him, she'd put him to bed. It wasn't worth it, if even he wasn't concerned about his suffering. "For you, I left a paradise for you!" the saint said, crying. It wasn't worth it. "Someone once told me, 'take care of yourself!'" he said, explaining to the saint. "Where I come from that means take a hike. Now, you see, I have to take care of myself, and someone writes that he was right." He was crying: "You are good, you don't have a home, you approve of doors only when they're a game. I want to go back to my coffin. It's true, you're the only one who can visit me, because you don't come through the window or through the door, and not even from the roof or through the chimney. When you pass by, the air is still. You endure in the name of the heavens, and I in the name of the void. There exist those who believe in you, and those who seek me out. You organized a party in your heavens. They won't come because they're afraid of dying. They'll find me out of curiosity. I endure, like a sketch on an ancient vase. We'd need too many specialists. These are sorrows from long ago. I'm talking to you, because it's impossible to talk to them. They dig to steal, not knowing that it would only take a breath of air to lose me. Like I told you: I lived, now she's dead. What do you want me to do with a miracle?" In reality, he was lying on the bed. The Saint had disappeared at an unconscious gesture from him, more specifically like a dead pharaoh, incorruptible, who rejects the offer of a Christian resurrection with a wave of his hand.

"Come on, come on, get up!" Even if he'd had a superficial friend, who'd come by to pick him up, say it, he probably wouldn't have ever gotten up. But the throngs of people, yes, they would've been able to approach his bed, in order to learn a little something about his life, outdated, like the word of God, too bad if made flesh. His Crusade was a strange one. It wasn't enough to flee from himself, to threaten his own body. He wasn't afraid of blackmail. He had to lose himself, is that it? Yes, yes, yes, without a doubt. But, for now, let him rest. Tomorrow & tomorrow & tomorrow, for a month, he'd have nothing else to do. He poured himself a Pernod, 90 proof, and didn't sleep. He told a disciple to open the bottom drawer of that icon. Begone! The seemingly most zealous one rushed over to it.

"Not the letters!" he sent another one to tell him, "not the letters!" Right there, if he were to look carefully, there should be a particular photo, among a bunch of others, of her. In costume, it would be easy to tell her apart, one time she'd volunteered to make an appearance in one of his performances. Not the one of her with the roses, and not the one with the lion at the zoo. It should show her with her face covered in markings. They both told him that they couldn't find it. So, they should help him up. Actually, they should stay right where they were. He'd do it himself; in any case, it was useless. He stood up, unsteady, but he made it to the icon. Looking elsewhere, among the anxious throng, perhaps he found that photo by feeling around for it and put it on the table, at a slant, leaning on the bottle of pure alcohol. Then, faltering, he went back to bed. He charged a disciple at his sickbed with informing the throng about that rite's propitiatory phase. All of them, by the thousands, would have to stare at that portrait for an hour, in silence and devotion, before learning something about him, the few monosyllables that the maestro, indisposed, was capable of uttering. A mute hour passed, without a clock. He was measuring the time by the diminishing liquid in the bottle that was within reach, calculating one minute less for every five, the time it took to modify the gradation. The hour was up. The faith of all those people wouldn't have lasted longer than that. "Margherita, Margherita..."

he said, calling out voicelessly, "I know how ridiculous what I'm about to ask you is. You need a miracle, another humiliation. She'd only need to take a train. I ask you this out of love: to be that woman who repented, like you, before they made you a saint. I know it's out of your way. Pretend you're taking a local train and then a taxi. Don't act as if you know how to find my place; convince yourself that you've never been here before. Ask about me when you arrive in town, give the wrong address, but apologize and ask my neighbors where exactly my address is, and when you're at the gate, call up to me. If I don't hear you, shake the iron grating. That way it'll seem unexpected. Dress differently than usual. You won't find a taxi at this time around here. You'll take a wagon or a horse-drawn cart. It'll be more unpredictable than flying. You'll see me before you see me, at the luminous waves of the lantern. Don't forget to beg the coachman to go slowly, because you feel sorry for the horse. I can wait a few more minutes for you. You'll be feeling worn out from the journey. You'll ask the driver how much farther it is. But, in the meanwhile, assuming that you'd gone most of the way by then, you'll catch glimpses of the sea, an ink stain, larger than your son's notebook. It will reassure you, that great unknown, motherly, like when you forgive him because he's still young. Be careful, Margherita, you'll have to believe you have a son. Beauty & stomach aches included, she suffered from liver problems, remember that. Change the roses on your cheeks, white roses if you have to look like her; under the pretext of using face powder in her stead, powder those reds, chosen by the virgins of Rudiae, on your cheeks, if in the alleyways, some papier-mâché artisans were to freeze in envy, having never seen you so pale. Talk about anything and everything with your guide, ask how many people live here, if they know me. Pretend that it's nighttime. You'll be shivering in your summer clothes, and be happy, because you'll be with me at dawn, and you know my habit of keeping the doors locked, like when it's dark. You know I'll let you sleep the first night. Call up to me when you're at the gate. I'll come get you with some of the youngest of my disciples. Perforce, you'll have a lot of luggage with you. One of my disciples will talk with the driver. The others will take care of the packages lined up on the perimeter wall. You mustn't kiss me. So that I'm not myself, I'll pretend to close the entrance gate, while you'll be staring at the house opposite. And there'll be a shattered moon, like a crystal from very high cutouts of the Moorish villa in India ink, finally a work of art. Without another way out, I'll show you the palm trees that, if only you knew, are all nested together, a deafening party all day long. You mustn't breathe a word. 'You know,' I'll resume seeming as if distracted, 'the neighbors are asking me to cut them down!' At this point, you'll have to rebel. Be careful, because she has a distinctive voice. You should conclude that they're stupid. I'll have said that to make you say something. It's been a long time since I've heard her voice. Tell me how our son is doing, even if you're barren, before you come into the house, if I forget to ask about him with all the excitement. You'll need to have procured a little blood, just a few drops, because maybe you'll have scratched yourself, perhaps while getting down from the cart. You mustn't notice my ulcerated body, but nor should you abstain from criticizing the excessiveness of my bandages, adding that I could easily consider myself lucky, since I never had to give birth. No, truly, I hadn't changed at all. You'll ask me for pure alcohol. I'll show you the little bottle behind the photograph. You'll want to treat your scratch by yourself. This will be the moment when you'll turn on the light, after having searched the whole room looking for the light switch. You'll complain about this tomb of a closed room. You'll open wide the windows, also raising the little bamboo curtains, and the Moorish villa, floating along, will invade the room. Go so far as to threaten that you'll sleep under the stars, if I don't put out those candles, revealing to me that you're not a saint, nor I thus embalmed, at least not as much as I'd have given you to believe. There, now we were starting to breathe. That room wasn't really a church, and even less a house, that room was a lighthouse, a consolation for sailors, and, for her part, she would've saved as many lives as possible, whether they were imaginary or not. Look, do you see that Moorish sail ship there, it may be the only one to have escaped at Lepanto, the thousand marvels of its marquetry work; it had to be seen & illuminated, who knows how much it had to cost! But, enjoy it, yes! Then you'll remind me that you've traveled, that you would like to get up early tomorrow, that you came to get some sun. Forgive me in advance if I sometimes step on your foot. It'll be to remind you to play your part, because, being so close to me, you might make her go crazy, by forgetting yourself and caress me or by throwing your arms around my neck. If I ask you, "do you want to play cards?" you'll say you're not in the mood. I know how much you like this particular game, and so it could make you give yourself away. You need to tell me no, is that understood? If, on the other hand, she'll be oddly in the mood for it, then you can accept, but do it in such a way that I won't notice. You can give me a signal, in the most difficult moments, or prompt me, but not when we're facing each other. Whatever you have to say to me, say it to me in the mirror."

At around two o'clock in the morning, a wagon stopped in front of his gate. He ran to the bathroom. He covered himself in very dark greasepaint, primarily to make sure the driver wouldn't notice him. He was naked, though bandaged. He put on a dressing gown and approached the convoy in the street. He'd have liked to help her down, but preferred to stay to the side, in any case away from the street light, also because the driver had gotten there first. He pretended, however, to move a step forward, in reality it was too far to attempt it, toward the luggage, which was forcefully taken away from him by that Cyrenean unconsciousness of his. They hadn't exchanged greetings when they saw each other. She had her back turned to him, right under the street light. She'd taken a make-up mirror from a traveling bag, intent on freshening up her make-up. He approached her, complicit, murmuring to her: "Don't worry, it's perfect, no need to fuss over it." "The things I have to do!" she said, mumbling with her mouth open, tense, tormented by the lip liner pencil's nervousness, "I'm pretty sure I've become an idiot!" "Be quiet!" He whistled at her, when he saw that the driver was coming back. "This is for you!" he said when the driver approached him, sliding a fistful of money in his hand. The wagon got on its way and turned the corner. At that moment, they looked at each other in the eyes, dumbstruck. She was about to smile at him, but instead she lowered her eyes on her bag. "What a mess!" she said, "All those jolts, I've never seen a street with so many humps like that!" They got on their way. She went first. He was limping a meter behind her: "Don't do anything stupid now; when you're at the door, I'll be the one to take the lead, is that understood?" She squeezed his hand, as if to say she'd heard him. "It's early, don't go overboard!" he said, imploring like a viper. She held his hand even tighter. "Are you crazy?!" He freed his hand, "if you turn your back to me, that will mean that you can speak freely." "All right!" the Saint said, groaning. They stopped at the entrance to the kitchen with the door wide open and blocked by the luggage. When he bent down, he brushed against her hair. She exposed her throat, looking at the terraces in a semi-circle, and he kept touching her lightly, her throat, her breasts, above her belly, she was wearing silk, until he let himself fall to his knees. Touching the ground, his wounds tore him apart more than a little and then, when he found himself down on the floor like that, he lifted up a suitcase: "It's heavy," he said happily, and not being able to lift it, "Wanna bet that she'll stay here forever?!" But he succeeded, nevertheless, and throwing his weight into it, he let it climb like a goat up onto the table. He turned to lift another large bag that was at his feet, and, noticing that she was looking up at the sky, he whispered: "I'd like to know what you put in this one!" She was more worried than she was contemplative, so much so that she turned around tired or angry, he never knew which one: "Aren't there any lights?!" she asked, staring at him. "Of course, dear; what made you think there weren't any lights?" He thought about how much trouble she could've saved him, then and there. She offered him her profile, with a huff, leaning against the archway, she was looking at herself in the window panes of the half door in front of her. So, he stepped on her foot. Then he flicked on the light switch. He pulled her inside with a jerk and slammed the door closed. The kitchen was yellow. Seeing that she was sitting down, he affectionately invited her to follow him: "The other room, let's go in the other room. It's hot in here, don't you think? I imagine you'd like something to drink, come on, let's go!" She nodded, following him naturally. "Why don't you turn on the light in here, too? Let's turn on the lights everywhere. I want to see the house!" She was expressing her wishes. Her guide bit his tongue. It was madness. She wanted to see him dead. But he carried out her wishes. They found themselves in the entryway. "Is it just me, or is this part of the house a little sad?" she asked, regretfully. He replied that no; that it wasn't just her, that he, from day one, thought only of destroying that entryway. In fact, it was the saddest part of the house. "May I turn off the kitchen light, eh?" he asked imploringly. He noticed her wilted smile, while she was saying, "leave it on, please," stopping him in mid-sentence, "let me see the rest first!" So, he stepped on her foot again, this time while cursing. When he'd turned around, she'd gone into the other room on her own. He caught up with her in the throes of terror. Too late. The light was on, the balcony, the sound of the sea, even the lamp on the veranda. Exasperated, swallowing nasty insults, he'd been about to slap her, but finding her facing him with, "it's been a long time, hasn't it, since we last saw each other?!," he ended that trajectory on himself, by swatting a mosquito: "there are a lot of them!" on his neck, on the exact spot of his most grievous wounds. His eyes sprouted two tears. He leaned against a chair to keep from fainting. Still, in that very same instant, having thrust one foot out from the urn toward "It's so beautiful from here!" a violent slap reached her. She turned around, moving her nostrils. That wax smell would've driven her crazy. Vindictive, she started tidying up, by taking the geraniums out of the vase; the water needed changing. She went to & from the bathroom. He, who, on one side, had opened his eyes wide in the mirror, was observing as if hallucinating the buds of his red wounds blossoming, expanding on the canvas of bandages, especially carnations, and two dahlias on his knees.

Why was he letting them do it? He, who had such a friend, such a lover!

Meanwhile, she was busying herself. She'd taken her clothes off so they wouldn't get dirty. She'd put on one of his dressing gowns. Whenever she happened to be at striking distance in the mirror, he would grimace repeatedly, in an attempt to communicate something to her, "Rita! Rita!" calling her voicelessly, "Rita" or cursing. It wasn't easy for them to understand each other, because she never stayed in one place for more than a second. Here, now it was more likely, because, being busy with reorganizing *Ursa Minor*, she was better framed in the mirror. "Do you want me to change your bandages?" She tried to get him to understand, having noticed that he was bleeding. For his part, entirely occupied in getting her to stop, he couldn't understand her and preferred to confront her, turning around: "Please don't, dear," enamored, "you must be tired!" Her response was: "Forgive me, someone may think I don't desire you. Isn't that right?" But she was joking. That wouldn't be like her. Without a doubt, the Saint was exaggerating. She was, perhaps, taking advantage of the weapon with which he himself had armed her in order to mar his memory of her, and that frightened him. He should've expected it. She'd perfectly captured those features, her face, her lips, a true miracle. Only in the depths of her eyes did she ill-conceal a jealous difference, enough to arouse his suspicion. It was human nature, indisputably feminine. If he'd reversed the roles, were that even possible, the unthinkable would've happened by then. He should've been happy for that. It was a miracle that he could spy on her, to see that even between the flashes of a celestial generosity, she cared about him, up to the point of jeopardizing an entire paradise. More arrogant than a Homeric mortal, he'd disregard the favors of a goddess, to alleviate the subjugation of his past. We can assume, precisely while he was thinking about that, the Saint was also thinking about it, and for that reason his beloved approached the walled-up space, and refusing to allow herself to be dissuaded for anything in this world, she opened her arms a meter wide and moved that entire construction, as if it had been a panel placed randomly on the window. She deployed the bamboo sail in the starry night, and the Moorish villa "it's so beauuutiiiffful" appeared as if enchanted. The Turks! He'd have liked to warn her, but it was too late. But if that angel were to turn its back on him, then he wouldn't have time to strike it, and if it were to face him, in defiance, his heart would break. Among other things, the infidels could not only nose around now, but they could also see him. Seeing him would be tantamount to reporting him. Oh my God, what to do? If she were to stare at him, and he at her, there would be two different loves for each eye! He hurried over to her, embracing her, while crying hot tears. He was holding her tight, kissing her, and she him, "You're here!" he said, raving, "You came back!" He was losing himself in her hair, chasing after himself under the Muslim arches, sliding his lips on her throat, in raptures, between her breasts and the domes, his hands two butterflies dying inside a hot wave, deranged, clinging to his true and to his false self, the arabesques, the spires, and the wounds, the vanished frescoes, alive, consisting of his ruin, from a fever obtained by magic, an ideal reality, including the deceit, taking advantage, oblivious, as if blood, using the magic spell that his lover had tempered for that carnal embrace to be possible, calling her all the way to the sea.

"I've lost my mind! I've lost my mind!" It wasn't enough for him to say it. He embraced her, also to prevent the other one from another kind of zeal. He was embracing both of them, infinite, nailed to the windowsill, perhaps by myriads of Turkish arrows. The Saint, in the throes of euphoria, or, in an obscene performance, in the throes of the most tormented jealousy, now seemed to be on top of herself, and that burning monster was fondling both her & the beast, brushing against a third, unnamable, animal. And, in fact, that fairy, fearing at times the confusion, was making use of the tangle, to hang on more tightly to her sin, &, at the same time, to lessen it, by bumping into his wounds, torturing him, and that head of his, lost in her undressed body, over her shoulders, was going round & round in an infinity of "It's over!" He was stepping on her feet, as if to say "I get it; I won't ever do it again. Let me do it." They were stepping on each other. The bandages on his ankles had loosened in the brutality of that carnal embrace. He was completely enveloped in it, covered in blood from an unstoppable hemorrhage.

Inexplicably, they detached themselves from one another, just like that, destroyed and scattered across the floor. There was a decomposition that would've been madness to reconstruct. Instead, diabolical, they recomposed themselves, starting with the Saint. She helped him get up. She told him to go look at himself in the mirror. At this point, they didn't see each other. "You see!" he said imitating her tone. "How can I trust you?!"

Miraculously, she was still able to maintain the other face, "You should take a bath," she said to him, after he'd turned around. "You know what, I should, too; I'm still covered in all that dust from the trip." It wasn't up for debate, and she slid into granting her wish. "Come here, it's ready!" she said, calling out to him from a distance. He followed her. It was a spacious bathtub. They got into the tub together. Now, he was able to see her whole body. It was extraordinary! Not only was the face indisputably hers, but also a great deal of illustrious love, subjugated to a terranean weakness, had almost reproduced the Saint's body: her figure certainly less slender, her protruding tummy, her ruddy nipples on swollen breasts, her head of copper, her hips as if suddenly cropped.

Stuck in pinkish water turned red, the slaves and the poets liberated, alone in his house on the Aventine Hill, in the honorable sweetness of a tub filled with blood, a lover was looking after his self-regard, having just cut his wrists, cradled in Venus's arms, raising glances at belfries and spires, if the skin were to emerge, chills at a misty, Gothic morning to come. She was thinking back on the day that they killed her, and him loving her again, more than it showed. The wind was kicking up, a hot wind, and, on the walls of the bathroom, the palm trees were swinging, black, at the vanishing moon.

A little later, they were all sitting around the table, all four of them: him and the Saint, along with the memory of her and the memory of him. All four of them were sitting around the table.

"I'm exceptionally in the mood for a game of cards this evening," the Saint said, shuffling the cards. "The two of us will play together," she proclaimed toward the balcony. Having not heard a reply to her plan, she added in exasperation, "Is that clear?!" Here, she stepped decisively on his foot. Or, perhaps, she'd intended to address the game's couples from a vertiginous height, operatic, ruthless. "We're together, the two of us!" she said, explaining, in simple terms, all the while looking at herself in the mirror. "Or, would you rather not?!" But of course, it was clear, a table of four, two appearances defying two realities. "You're here and you're there, you get it?" she said finally, believing to have made herself clear. "I'll be here, and the signorina will be there. Or maybe that doesn't work for you?" Even this coda, this checking in with him, after having invented that monstrous arrangement herself, this coda really annoyed him. Especially since, looking him in the eye, she said: "It works for me!" He was the only one being difficult. "It's been such a long time since I've played!" she said, frontally, in a fearful confession. "It doesn't matter!" she said, turning to the bed, and he said, "it doesn't matter, my dear, we're all friends here, or at least I hope we are!" Then, she stepped on his foot. "Let's change the rule!" he said, in pain, looking around on the floor, as if searching for a fallen card, but impressed by the inventive eventuality of that celestial imagination. "Or maybe not, forgive me!" he said, correcting himself. "Your turn!" said the Saint, handing over the deck to him, "shuffle them, if you like!" There was little to shuffle. He quickly started dealing the cards, as if they were on fire. The Saint, completely at ease, found herself with five cards in her right hand and the same number in her left hand. He thought he might do the same. She, curly-haired, with her hair still wet, was smiling slyly at him just then. "What are you doing? Are you looking at the cards?" the Saint asked, shouting and looking up at the ceiling. Interdicted, he asked her for an explanation with his foot. "Those are the dead man's cards!" she said in no uncertain terms, "Yours are the other ones!" The dead man was at the head of the table with his back to the mirror. "That's the fun of the game," the fairy said, "none of us three must see them!"

Now, he began to understand, and he wasn't happy about it. The witch was controlling his double, reading his part, and she knew all her opponents' cards. But he didn't. Because the dead man was sitting to his left. Come on, it was all too logical that he should be informed, if he'd be playing next! He was about to say to her, "If you can see his...," but then, feeling like he was being watched, he modified it to say: "You? What do you think about it?" She started to say in a faint voice, "Here...," and then, searching for a rock in her shoes, "Here there's fuck all!" she said, articulating rudely. Then, having collected herself, turning to smile at him, she admitted: "It would seem that the lady is right!" "It's the game!" the Saint said, for clarity's sake, while looking everywhere for her cigarettes, "it's the game!" Yes, but it was precisely the game that didn't convince him, and that didn't amuse him, and that annoyed him to such an extent that it seemed as though the dead man was saying to him, "Send the women away, we'll play, just the two of us, send them away!" Why send both of them away? The only one who was bothering him was that lady. Indeed!

Margherita can mean "sweet" without signifying "instrumental." Her name, if anything, can be translated as "present," or even "elsewhere." But: "Let's get going!" she said, spurring on the game, "who's turn is it?"

"I don't know, I wasn't paying attention!" he said, apologetically. The Saint had clearly decided to drive him mad. Tarantismized in an ever-changing tic, like an accelerated film reel, she'd be looking at him, or not, crying and smiling, putting a card down with her left hand and picking it up with another, as if a shovel, in her right hand, smiling and crying, looking at him, or not, undoubtedly excited, yelling: "Let's start over, let's start over, there's a card missing!" It seemed as though she wanted to send him signals, or tell him which cards to play, or she'd even go so far as to cheat. And cheat she most certainly did. She was taking advantage of the two sexes, both of them feminine, that he, himself, had entrusted to her. She'd complain for both of them, insult him, then soften, everything multiplied. In the meantime, his mood would bounce who knows where. In the end, her voice would function like a superimposition. She'd say, simultaneously, "I'm gonna go; it's late!" and, "I'd like to sleep, too!" deforming her face's features, by then undecipherable, dangerous, where one expression would give rise to yet another, until it became a pyramid, a mosaic of conflicting gestures, amassed from either folly or unbridled passion. She gathered up all the cards in a frenzy and put them back in their box, while planning: "Will you come with me to the sea tomorrow?" Just like that.

"Send them away, we'll play, just the two of us!" He thought back on the dead man's words. He'd gotten up and the ruinous allure of that ulcerated body in the mirror had nearly ignited an insurrection of reproaches from within. He released himself, like an indolent castellan, to avoid succumbing to his duties, we won't say military duties, so social duties, but of the fiefdom, a guarantee of the work of others and also of his own; like how things once were, he'd dismissed her, stating: "But you are so much sweeter when you know not to distract me." Did anything ever change? Never so much as now, his quotidian role, far from determining the choice as of yet, would suggest he go on a journey of idolatry, one that would remain forever motionless, demonstrating the exceptional nature of his self-regard. In any event, it would've happened indirectly that the discomfort of his pain would induce him to take off from his swollen fingers the most recent, worthless rings, showing him what one can clothe a nude with, without resorting to garments, or to jewels, or to metaphors. "Send them away, we'll play, just the two of us! You think it makes no difference that they stay, is that it? Now is not the time to exaggerate!" the dead man's ghost said, admonishing him, "you know, physiologically speaking!" Then, he started citing phrases to him from his diary, annotations that not even the author would've remembered so perfectly. "They're going!" that specter revealed to him, "they're either going to go or stay, depending on if you pretend to move or not. There's only one way, yours, to meet halfway. Exactly the opposite of meeting. You see? It's a game of R's. What do you want to represent your perversion, outside of an onomatopoeic probability? It's not by trying to be clever that you'll become an idiot. Send them away! Are you missing an opportunity, or not? This way, they'll bestow on you a beautiful castle where it is required to move around without thinking. This divine, unconscious movement signifies when she, for example, had decided to come to visit you on the spur of the moment. You'll be in your favorite cage, every visit a failed poem. Note that your conversation with her, when she'll be close to the bars, will be about courtesies, about the reasons you stopped writing to her, about how much money is needed, about a whole vague Arcadia of problems that your animalistic midday wouldn't know how to solve. But, what do you want to do now?"

The dead man still hadn't left the table. The Saint had put her silk dress back on, while he, taking advantage of a moment, unobserved, permitted himself to hide under the bed. It would've been interesting to observe them together, the Saint wearing a mask and that garrulous dead man. Lying on the floor like that, his wounds were particularly hurting him. Yet that was nothing next to facing the surprise that, while somewhat uneasily crouched in this way, instead of listening, he was seeing. He tried to avert his eyes, but he was still seeing. He was seeing the same thing everywhere. Even the dead man, who'd had, up until then, the good taste to admonish him, being careful not to assume a figure, was precisely his alter ego, unlike him, better dressed, in evening wear, all in black, wearing cologne, his fingers completely covered in rings. He was offering cigarettes, pouring drinks, courting, in spite of everything, the Saint, who, for her part, was allowing herself to be taken in by him. "Margherita!" he was saying, whispering indignantly from under the bed, "Margherita!" In vain, no one would hear him, also because the Saint, strangely, had at this point taken on all of her features, of his her, without a single trace of holiness. If anything, humble, he had to hope for a lacuna, the emptiness of a moment when she'd have betrayed herself. There they were, facing each other, discussing things, perhaps because, without her evil presence, the deceit would become truth. What would become of him, if he'd hate himself from that moment on? But, of course, that elegance wasn't new to him: the tie was one of his ties, and he'd only ever worn the cufflinks in Florence. What about her? What more could be added? Even traces of psoriasis on the skin. He hadn't noticed them during the card game. The dead man was he who, being dead, was healed. Not even a scratch on him. Those two nightmares started playing. Not at cards anymore. They were talking, both of them obstinate, but him, he'd never been so deaf; he could only follow what they were saying by interpreting their hand gestures, if he succeeded, that is. Saint Margherita, or she, stood up and started turning everything upside down everywhere. She came back, placing an enormous chess board on the table. "The pieces are missing," he thought, intrigued, under the bed. It was true, they weren't there; he'd forgotten them in Naples the previous year. The two mimes hadn't given it a thought. They confabulated for a long time, negotiating. "Why can't I hear?" He was the only one talking to himself. Then he saw that both of them were rummaging around: he in his pockets and she in her purse, undoubtedly looking for some facsimiles of the pieces. The gentleman knight pulled out several little objects: a withered carnation that he placed in the king's square and a cigar lighter in the queen's. A little tube of Veramon aspirin and another tube of deodorant in place of the bishops. The knights, two telephone tokens and, maximum defense, the castles, two small cylindrical packets of certain condoms. On the other side, so great was the disproportion of the chess board, the Saint had also pulled out more than one object at random: two different tubes of lipstick, two balled-up letters, two souvenir cigarette lighters, and two make-up pencil stubs. In the meantime, her adversary had created a vanguard of pawns made from various cigarette butts, that the Saint immediately cleared off the board, since she was undoubtedly allergic to the smell, and replaced them with cotton balls on her adversary's field and birth control pills in her own. "Checkmate! Checkmate!" she said, screaming at the top of her lungs, so loudly that even he heard it, and this before they'd even started the game. The gentleman knight was holding onto her wrist, perhaps indicating to her another path to salvation, because she insisted on moving the cosmetics, especially the tallest one, by one square back. "I don't want to look!" said the lady, yelling implausibly, while freeing herself. There it was, he'd heard her. "I lost, and that's that!" she said, but to say that she was raving, that she'd gone mad, would be putting it lightly. "Soon, when East will turn white this useless flicker of fireflies, these two sprites will disperse, & I'll be in jail!" Curled up, that was the only thing he feared. A patron of Jacobean festivals, he who had sworn to serve his king! He would've also liked to get out from under the bed, but he wasn't able to. He couldn't get on his knees, not so much because of his wounds, but because the space was too low for him to do so. He couldn't crawl because he was one big sore. Nor could he start yelling, since he'd lost his voice. Thus sacrificed, solutions such as hanging himself or throwing himself off the balcony would've seemed ethereal to him. There exists a dying of rage, but it's a figure of speech.

Many centuries ago, a predicament like this one would've amused him, and then annoyed him. He'd have said, "Let's get going!" and she, docile, would've followed him. They never would've gotten this far. "Checkmate! Checkmate!" How happy she was to have finished the game! A pang in his heart told him that the lady had turned on the light in the hall. On the threshold, the door open, they were separating. "I love him and I don't love him!" she said, confiding in the dead man. "Tomorrow morning, at ten o'clock, you'll come pick me up, right? Thanks for this evening. Good night!" She, the spitting image of her, went back to the room, undressing along the way. She joined him, completely naked, under the bed: "What do you think, shall we go up top?" she asked and threw her arms around him. "Rita, Rita!" "You're calling me Rita now?!" she said with indignation. "Who's this Rita?" She detached herself from him and got up on the bed to sleep. She turned on the lamp on the bedside table, nervously leafing through a magazine: "I'm leaving tomorrow!" interspersing sulkily, "I'm leaving tomorrow!" she said, throwing away a cigarette she'd just lit. He picked it up & started smoking it. What was happening? "You only think about one thing!" she said, reproaching him & lighting another cigarette. "You think the dead man is courting me. You're jealous, clearly. But I'll make you pay for this... You could've..." Then, she started to cry. Lacerating himself, he inched away from there, now under the table. "You're a demon!" she said, yelling & staring straight at him. "If she's staring, then it's true," he said to himself, "or, at the very least, it's true that she is the one saying it to me!" "Get out of here, you make my skin crawl! I'm afraid to show my body to a depraved beast like you!" Either the Saint was truly good, or she was anything but a Saint. In any event, she was naked, out of breath, and agitated: "Come here, you idiot; it doesn't mean wounded, you know? Come here, I'm cold, hold me, I curse the day I met you!" She called him an idiot. One day everyone would call him that. Sooner or later they would realize it! But there was still time! She was blessed with a peculiar sort of intuition. "Yes, yessss," he said, murmuring, while climbing up onto the bed. They kissed each other all over for a long time. They were raving, insulting each other undefinedly. He, agonizing in his saliva, was mumbling, understood: "everywhere." She, being more geometric, as if transmitting while drowning, was confessing, "Everyone's, everyone's!" It was dawn. "You know," he said, kissing her foot, "in the end, everything is a question of money!..." He felt machine-gunned by a laugh. Her figure leapt to her feet, having reclaimed the Saint's face, by now half-dressed, and presently intent on recovering all of her ex-votos. "Five centuries ago, in Otranto," she said to him icily, while buttoning up her dress, "you would've liked to die. Now, you want to live, isn't that right? This tournament of yours is rigged. Don't count on my loyalty anymore. Instead, think about paying your phone bill! This luxury of blood doesn't suit you. The evil doesn't reside in the fact that you, believing me to be a whore, tried to make me your faithful sycophant, since this was what I was hoping for you when I first saw you from my altar. The incense must've blinded me. The evil resides in the poor young man that you are. All the worse for you, if you're aware of it. Heaven is everything you don't touch even if you desire it the most. But you don't pray. You don't know how to desire, nor do you know how to touch. You see everything and can't transform anything. Would you like to come with me? They won't let you in. It's a miracle that they tolerate me. I'm still admitted due to my past merits. It would take you some kind of barbarism, and luckily those don't happen anymore!"

What was she talking about? She wasn't expecting, by any chance, that she could make him believe that the Moorish villa was, as they say, from the period, or was she? That piece of architecture was a fake. There was really no need to be an expert on it. It was designed and built in the early 1900s, come on! The slaves simply didn't know what they were doing. The owners had wanted it to resemble one. Come on. It was like a reflection in water. It emerged. It wasn't put to the test. It was outdated kitsch. Why did that have to be a clue? Like forbidding someone from singing because he is tone-deaf! Let him sing, just let him sing! Thus, they built it vertically on the cliff-side, like a sin that would serve as an example for others to avoid. Like an unbridled dance of naked young women in Salem, reproduced in a church, so that all the devoted virgins, including the dancers, would never even think of trying it. An infinity of Moorish arches. First you see them, and then you pass through them. He, who'd had tried his hand at masonry, was aware of the effort when dealing with tuff upon tuff. He wouldn't have raised any objections.

There are streets everywhere that are more respected than others. That castle is even habitable. Like how a dream foresees the waking — that was how the founders had wanted it — as if to say that, here, the Turks certainly wouldn't have dared to build a villa. Nevertheless, a Moorish castle exists. But what was it doing?

Does it recall the billowing sails with the half-moons? Not at all. Not up for sale, it sells itself. It contemplates even the briny sea, and it abhors the neighboring houses, as if a white bandage tossed away, caught here and there on the palms, reused by the westerly wind that makes of it a belvedere parapet, repaying the kneeling pine grove. And that singular error of the domes stands out, thus setting itself free from an entire southern Italian truth. Humped arches, camels dead on their feet, terrified by the desert of

an infinite sea. Bringing up the rear of this pointless caravan, petrified, a canopy that won't leave. Because it has to live. Much more than men and beasts.
It's capable of anything, even of drinking sea water.
So, it isn't unreasonable to ask yourself how thirsty
would it be?

Little kids from summer camp were walking in
line, under his windows, at dawn. Right when he was
about to go to bed. He calmed himself down. He went
to take a look. "It's unbelievable," he said, when he saw
them, "starting so young!" "Ah, but they have to be
followed closely...!" He stumbled all the way into the
bathroom and cleaned himself up.

Crossing the hall, he pretended he was being ha-
rassed, "Give him something to eat!" he said, proclaiming, "once I've taught him to read properly, you'll
see, he'll sleep!"

He entered the classroom; never so unwilling. He
opened a drawer, on the exact opposite side of the urn.
He shuffled things around until he found a packet of
his containing elementary compositions. A bundle of
corrected homework.

"That's it, that's it," he said, avenging himself, by
changing the composition's topic with a copy paper
pencil. "Why get up so early in the morning?" Then he
crossed out the grades he'd received, writing in really
big letters "OFF TOPIC!"

At this point, the crowd was returning home. They'd gone to bed early. Those who understood the town's dialect listened. Would the news spread the next day, or not? It would, it would! When he'd forced himself to go to the window, an assistant on duty for the summer camp's innocent massacre, he'd actually noticed unusual hordes of people amassed around the fountains, two of them for the whole town, both of them visible. He'd guessed what those bees were buzzing about. It was far worse than usual. It was about a problem at the aqueduct. Not only were the pipes in the area affected, but all the lines in the region. "Thank God they're made of iron," he said to himself. The Apulian aqueduct without water. Incredible! Then he remembered, "There's a well in the courtyard."

These multitudes that came running to listen to me are no longer thirsty in a material sense, since, having passed away, they no longer drink. He would call having passed away those who existed only in his mind. Those devotees of his weren't dead, because they were too attached to the future. In this day and age, what could possibly be done with this accidental present? As for the Turks, there were only two routes: one north to Gargano, and the other to their homeland. The local authorities were doing their utmost to get the invaders to be patient, promising that it was only a question of a day, that there had been a technical problem, but they were prepared; let them sharpen their axes to distract themselves. If they were to have a head — everyone in town had one — then it was for them; they might at least try cutting it off, and drink the blood! Let them be satisfied with more. The less for that year was unlikely. They mustn't leave. They'd always had an imagination. If they were to leave, the tourist office would no longer intervene, like when it closed its eyes on Otranto's excesses 500 years ago. Additionally, there was a very good wine. The thermal baths wouldn't be open for a short period, that's all.

He was congratulating himself like a proprietor of a bed and breakfast, sitting on the bed and bouncing, boasting about the freshly laundered sheets, "What a great bed," he said, adding, "when had he ever slept this well?" Then, thinking back on his physical destruction, he closed his eyes to the father prior's words, who was saying to him: "And this isn't nothing! What matters most is how we are somewhere else!"

The monks had already rung the bell for matins while he was playing cards. These dings now are for the first mass. His hermitage was much more ahead of time. If he didn't heal, at least superficially, he wouldn't be able to appear in public. His skin was a perimeter wall. If, tomorrow, the police found themselves in danger near that monastery of his, imploring him "Let us in, for the love of God!" in no way would he have violated the rules of the seclusion.

It wasn't a cloister like the others, but a monstrous refuge of blind faith in themselves, a lazaretto where self-flagellation was a preventative therapy for the simplest temptations, such as, "shall we dance, signorina?," the meditation made obligatory from modesty, loving thy neighbor an uncertainty that, once admitted, would become more & more difficult to clarify later on. There was even a garden. They cultivated flowers like they avoided sin. They bent their backs, not so far as to heal, but far enough to arrive at the most elastic, pliable invulnerability.

In those cells, they only lied to God. Every now and then, over the centuries, the most bumbling one would become a saint. Charity, this sublime act of distancing oneself from it, piety, this certitude of recognizing in one's own reflected image the other infinity of the ruin, adopting a rhetorical form in the private notes in his diary, displaying, for those who would come after him, a clarity around his own doubts, up to the point of describing them with a pleasant assurance. At the temple, the priests, being knowledgeable on the entire 19th century, would've excommunicated him for the impiety of the perpetrated citations. They would've placed him facing the rite of mechanics, systematic humility, an amplification of well-being, recorded initially and then reproduced, minus the vanity of the pulpit.

They would've deplored that way of his of deciding on his own. Above all, they would've questioned his making an emotion out of the emergency. They weren't in agreement about the need for God, & not even about the god of necessity. They weren't in agreement about life, both the one we grasp at, and the one we suffer. They weren't inclined to forgive him for his fideistic past. In contrast to his novitiate, they belonged to a race of bored monks at the outposts of the nonexistent, shirking their duties for the purpose of imparting a mundane dogma to more distant countries, Lebanon, Albania, which they would be able to more or less distinguish, depending on if it was a clear day or not. With respect to the rules, they weren't worthy of depriving themselves of anything.

Someone was knocking on the door. He ran to the bathroom to lather his face and opened the door, a patch of sunlight, just enough for Mercury to throw, without any proof, a little envelope in one of his eyes. He detached the reception stub himself, autographed it and gave it back to the messenger. He opened it immediately. A check from his father. He followed the mailman for a moment, until he disappeared. He couldn't just show up at the bank, not with those marks on his face, let alone disguised in lather. He heard screaming in the courtyard, but it was joyful. Undoubtedly, a childlike jubilation. He thought about the previous night. He hurried down the stairs in the direction of the screaming, as if he were chasing a nightmare.

His courtyard was covered in moss, like a well, and only from the parapet above the roses could you comprehend its absolute bottom. It was impossible to discern all the angles from the loggias, only one at a time, ever-changing, depending on the position of the neighboring houses. To focus on its center, a curious person would've had to be everywhere at once. Therefore, someone could creep along the walls, all the while remaining invisible from the exterior. He was running as if he were running inside his house. Then, at the bottom of the stairs, approaching him, he saw a little boy, delirious with wonder at a butterfly's red and gold wings. They found themselves one in front of the other. Who knows why his nightmares were always so cheerful. Perhaps to frighten him even more. He nearly had to stop himself in midair to avoid running over that little event. At this point, the butterfly was transparent in the sun, as the little boy pointed at it. Irresponsible, he, too, looked at the azure vapor trail of a roaring jet engine in the cotton wool. They both looked at each other, disenchanted. He tried to reassure the boy, by letting him know that if his teeth hadn't been so dirty, he would've smiled more openly at him. But the little kid, now that the butterfly had vanished, greatly bewildered at the reality of someone else wounded in this way, burst out in hysterical tears, crying out a female name for help. Sure enough, he was saved by a teenage girl who, evidently, he was entrusted to and who was only now hurriedly coming down the spiral stone staircase, in pursuit of that object of which she had made herself responsible. She went to him, picked him up and held him tightly in her arms. She was definitely not his mother. She couldn't have been more than fifteen years old & the little boy not less than seven. He was as sure of that as he was that it wasn't yet ten o'clock in the morning. He remained still so that she wouldn't die. She was dressed in very light cotton, the color of the palm trees' tops broken-off in the air, matured to death from the sun's intensity. Underneath this image, nothing else presented itself, in his opinion, between the scratchy reverse side and her body. But there was nothing more intimate than this suspected absence of lace, some sweat wounds on how much divinity her breasts were still silencing in her dress; but very little, in truth, because he'd listened to all of it, and also because that little boy, grabbing on to her there, and receiving a kiss, had uncovered a nipple that she, in her distraction, didn't cover up immediately. And it didn't end there. That little heathen, unleashing a thousand gestures, exposed the other breast, too. He remembered that, when he was little more than a baby, he would occasionally stay behind in the church and, while the sexton was absorbed in snuffing out the candles, he would take advantage of that time to lift up the Madonnas' skirts and be astonished at running his hand along the easels all the way up to the knees, since they didn't resemble those of his mother. That very young woman — her gentle way of tending to one thing after another — she was trusting in the sun, like a little field church, unaware of everything among the wheat, and he was a whole flock of famished birds, suspended in the middle of this airy enchantment. He'd never undressed anything in his life with so much candor. She couldn't see him yet, since, blonder than a small rock of honey, she was helping that little boy to let him climb on her. Nor had he seen her face yet. Then, precisely toward this end, attempting to meet her without hands at the pinnacle of that amazement, the only thing left for him to do was to follow two small hands that were waving around in an aerial grasp and slipping from the domes' huge Moorish belly, a little infinity of attempts that dissolve themselves, that fall short, like snowflakes.

She went along with it, like a tree that ripens another fruit. The imp was screeching, oblivious, at the top of her neck, discovering the euphoria from his terror; his small foot, caught on either the hem or a cotton thread, had raised her dress up to her belly, revealing her to him just as he'd dreamed her to be, a layer of wet sugar, like on bread, and a tuft of ash-colored grass, dying between her thighs, to complicate a cunning pink riddle. That nymph didn't realize it, or at least not right away. But, while focusing on balancing that rascal's weight up on high, she was revealing her exposed graces in several sections of her thighs, and her tummy's trembling, that natural way of finding equilibrium by widening the gap between the thighs, was providing her with the initiative, aggravating the faunlike ambiguity of that obscene swallowing of his, the imbecile. He who was nearly about to cry at the thought that, even if he were to have looked up, it wouldn't have justified an erection. At that very moment, the dress's hem pulled out a white little sandal from Cupid. Still holding him in her arms, shifting him slightly from side to side, that attentive naiad bent down to pick it up, in such a way that her little cherub, the wrong way around, perhaps terrified to find himself upside-down, had only narrowly avoided pulling off her dress while hanging onto her. While bending down, she'd turned herself around. She found herself bent over, with her back to him, unexpected to the eyes of the wounded man, who was mummified by then. That imp settled in for a piggyback ride, urging her on mischievously, and, every time his patient beast of burden was about to recover the sandal, he only had to bounce a little above her nude and sweaty hips to make her lose it again. Thus, she was involuntarily showing herself from the other side. She had a sturdy body, turgid, roomy but not fat, imperfect, present, sin. But now, unlike a moment before, when she'd shown herself to him frontally, she was laughing a hot and labored laugh, amused by the impertinence of that, at this point, unbridled rider of hers. Assuming a permanent frown, he was standing there, like a Caryatid overburdened under the weight of the balconies in the air, where there was the possibility of seeing even more.

Now, peradventure, her clothing was completely covering her, and she was finally still. She looked off in the distance, here and there, everywhere, fixing her hair and fanning her slightly reddened youthful face. She wasn't aware of his presence: bandaged up like that, he most certainly wouldn't stand out on the whitewash, and she left, trotting along, a little tired, behind her piglet. He went backwards up the stairs and followed her until she was one with the oleanders. It was truly stupid to lose her, but climbing up to the terrace would've been even more idiotic. He was about to do it, when he caught a glimpse of them between the oriental arches, the Maenad and her little god, leaning on the caprices of the balustrade. He had the impression that they were pointing at him, or maybe not.

Entering the kitchen, he found the friar focused on making himself a good cup of coffee. "Father!" he said, shouting at him rudely, "I need you to leave me in peace this morning!" "Do I really!" the monk said, blaspheming between one gulp and another. "You have to tell me!" he said, pestering him, "you have to tell me!" "No! Not this time!" "Dirty pig!" spat the friar, burning himself, by emptying the cup on his face & then subsequently breaking it on his head. He flew into a rage, like a business partner. As a matter of fact, his eyes bloodshot, he was repeating, while biting his tongue: "I'm gonna destroy everything!" Threatening just that, he started throwing chairs, pots, and pans all over the place, and throwing stones at him, irrational. He'd undoubtedly gone mad. He lifted up his cassocks so that he could also kick the shelves. Luckily, there was also lighting & thunder outside, alongside alternating torrents of water, one of those unpredictable summer storms that covered up the scorn of that religious man, who, sharpening two large kitchen knives, was smiling a little at him, and also a little at the trickles running down the window panes, promising: "I'm not going to fly into a rage. Look over here instead!" Then, opening his arms, powerless, his eyes toward heaven, he was lamenting the mess of which he was the author. "It's your fault!" he said, calming down, "if you had only told me sooner... You know that I don't think, don't you? When I see that you are beyond grace, I go batshit crazy!"

He being stunned, or, if you like, penitent, fell to his knees at the other's feet. "Come on, come on! Get some other plates!" the friar said to him, sternly, ruffling his hair, "and then wash some of that ridiculous blood off. Ridiculous is just what we want. These kinds of aches heal in a day. But miracles disgust you…" He briefly interrupted himself to kill a fly. After, he tried to turn on the faucet: "Hand me a dish towel," he said, ordering him. He carried out the order, but the friar, blaspheming, delivered such a violent blow to the pipe that it broke apart, not near the faucet, but on the ceiling. The pipe swung back and forth for a second, still barely attached, & then crashed down onto the sink. A forceful jet of water from above began to flood the windowpanes. It was raining both inside & outside. "We need to do something," the friar said, "we can't reach it with the chair. Get it from there…!" he was yelling, bedeviling the table. "Let me do it, I'll do it…" he said, grabbing a chair that he was perhaps intending to put on the table, but the friar, at the end of his wits, bit his hand, barking his head off more than a rabid dog: "Don't touch that chair or I'll eat you!" He was exaggerating, so much so that, profanation or not, he was about to ring his neck. The friar was on the table in a single leap, trying his best to stanch the leak with a dish towel. That rag was too big. He reduced it into many pieces with his teeth, all of them far too small. "Hand me another one!" he said, shouting at him. He didn't understand because of the racket the water was making on the windows. "Pass me another dish towel so I can tear it in two!" he said, croaking.

In any case, it was useless. No kind of patch would've been able to withstand the pressure. He decided to shut off the water entirely. The father had hurt his finger, perhaps when he'd been busy on the table. He had other wounds on him, which was why the town considered him a saint. "Take this!" the sinner said, offering him one of his bandages. In return, the friar sent him a curse word. Then, he dipped a finger from his other hand in those red droplets and, nonchalantly, made himself two rosy cheeks out of them. "Look at that!" he said, proudly, as if he had just defeated a dragon, "me, I don't think about maidservants!" and then he wanted to "Turn on the lights!" He couldn't refuse.

There was at least an inch of water on the floor. The spices, the eggshells, the onion peels were already swimming around. "What will become of us!" the friar said, while looking down at his feet, "if we aren't able to get up a little higher!" He nodded his head. Then, he started preparing the sauce.

He was chopping up a carrot, grumbling, his voice monotonous and nasal: "You have to tell me every-thing, is that understood? Even if I whip you later on." "If I were to do this to you," he said after a bit, while pointing out the tomatoes to him and immersing them in hot oil, "then you'd have reason to fear me."

"I even taught you to drink. And yet, when I decid-ed to look after your soul, you used to like snow with mulled wine."

"We have exceptionally beautiful bodies," he said, licking the wooden spoon soaked in sauce, "think of the image that we imitate, and therefore, don't love anyone except yourself. Set the table! It's still raining, and the wind has kicked up. We'll drink a good cognac today. This meat has gone bad," he said, sniffing inside the package, "naturally: you eat so little; you'll end up letting yours get spoiled, too, but, thank God, you eat yours more often!"

Handing him a pot, he said: "Go to the well, and don't fill it up completely. After I've left, remember to call the plumber, even if it's not urgent. The water in the pipes was a reserve. It'll take them a long time to repair the problem at the aqueduct. Hurry up, I'm hungry."

That morning, the friar only gave him precise tasks, small services. Who knows what he was thinking. He had no idea. The same thing had happened to him on other occasions in the past, ever since the day when they'd left him to his own devices, to interpret, in his own way, his spiritual confessor's remarks by turning them upside down. He went down to the well, in the courtyard, in the downpour. The gutters, riddled by the hail and shaken by the wind, were groaning, and the palm trees were bending over so low that they were nearly throwing themselves at the windows to spy on them. He went back up the stairs, running, with the overflowing pot on his head, protecting himself from what other dangers he may encounter, quickly turning toward the Turkish castle that insisted on carrying on with the performance, regardless of the bad weather. He went back into the kitchen, completely soaked. "Wonderful," the friar said, "I'll take it from here," taking the pot from him. "That's a lot, it's too much," and then he dumped a good half of it on the floor. "I'd advise you to take off those wet clothes, otherwise you're likely to catch cold. In fact, do it now. Or, go naked if you like. You know how happy that makes me. Get a move on and try to mop up this water the best you can, while I take care of the pasta." He did as he was told. "You know what?" the cook said, resuming, "You know what? I'm almost in the mood to joke around today. It must be this foul weather. Let's play a game, ok? We'll play to amuse ourselves while we work: whenever lightning flashes, you'll kiss one of my hands, and I'll pull it away, then you, without losing heart, will kiss my other hand, and that is when I'll allow it. Got it?" This wasn't the first time that the holy man had suggested diversions like these to him. "I'm happy," the friar said, in conclusion, "also because there's no one else here, and also because you'll tell me everything, after we've eaten, over coffee. There, you see what I'm like, if I think back on it, if I think back on how you didn't want to tell me about it before, this time, no, you told me, I'm overtaken by desire to destroy everything again." In the meantime, he was busy, while he, for his part, was doing his best to dry the remaining puddles on the floor. "Please, do it quickly!" the friar said, spurring him on, "do it quickly, otherwise, I'll make ice out of this damned water and then I'll crush it with a hammer." In conclusion, he pronounced forcefully: "Stay away from whores!" "She's not a whore!" he said, reiterating, and this time it was he who was being forceful: "You're mistaken, or you want to be mistaken, because you saw everything with your own eyes from the balcony, everything you might want me to tell you. She's only a child…" When he heard that last word, the friar appeared to be tarantismized. Screaming his head off like a possessed man, he got up on the table, first dancing like a devil, and then doing high jumps, trying to touch the ceiling with his head. He soared in the air, hoping to reach the closet. He didn't know how to fly either. He fell back down on his butt badly, but on a chair. "Did you see that?" he said, in reality he'd become an idiot, but pretending to be calm and pensive, "We're made for thinking. It's useless for us to make mistakes. Did someone knock on the door? I heard the doorbell!" "No," he replied, "the power is out. Probably due to the storm." "Well then, the water's boiling, let's cook the pasta. How hungry are you?" He admitted that he was very hungry. The friar grabbed a package of spaghetti from a shelf. Suddenly, the other one grabbed his hand. Lightning was flashing outside. "What are you doing? Why do you want to take it away from me? Have you lost your mind? So, we'll eat this evening!" He would often forget the games that he himself had established. So, he took hold of his other hand to kiss it, holding it involuntarily firmly on the red-hot saucepan. The friar, wild with rage, took a bite from a wheel of hard cheese. Then, tossing the spaghetti in the steam: "These things," he said to him, with a full mouth, "you can't do them with children; with whores it's likely, but you can't take advantage of them as you do of me!" Upon which, he started grating the cheese, announcing to him: "You do know, don't you, that I've prepared a wonderful evening for you? There's going to be a full moon tonight. This downpour will let up, and when the storm clouds clear, you'll go on a little boat ride with the Saint." "I don't want to; I have a lot to do!" he said, making himself a cocktail. "That Saint is a woman!" the friar said, patiently reiterating, "and that may be useful to you in the end. You should cherish this friendship. Just think what you'll save on telephone calls alone. She nursed all your unnamable maladies!" "Healed, not nursed!" the other said, clarifying, "it's different. Hopeless cases are her thing. She gets bored, up there, where she resides."

"For her, the only way to lose herself is to waste time with me. Instead of that, you know, I'm fairly sure that I'll die in a few days, or I may even be just fine. In either case, it'll be over between us. If I die, they won't

allow her to resuscitate me. If I live, she'll fall out of
love with me." "Then you must know," the friar said,
intervening, while serving the pasta, "You must know
that I won't allow it. I'll become your enemy. Bear in
mind that I'll be on my way one of these days. I'll leave
you, and that will be worse. So, then, all you'll have
left is to resemble me. Resemble, what an ugly word!
But not really. I eat. We eat. People like us conjugate
ourselves; we don't decline ourselves."

They were eating, for real. "I'll dedicate my wounds
to whomever I please," he said into his plate. The friar
was gesturing no with his finger, because a mouth-
ful of food had gone down the wrong way. "Look," he
said, after having emptied an entire beer stein full of
wine, "if it were true, then these cheap amusements
of yours should hang from you like earrings. But you
plunge this bauble into the flesh…" "What business
is it of yours how I use it?" the other one said, spitting it out in a single breath." "You see?" the friar said,
syllabifying, while biting his lower lip, "you want to
lead me to gradually recognize as ordained by heaven
the encounter with that scullery maid: you want to go
out with her on horseback at night, telling her about
yourself. You'll go on an amorous swim together, and
thus far, there wouldn't be any harm done. The ma-
cabre will be in something else, that is, that you'll tell
her the whole truth. Naturally, she won't understand.
But you will. And that wouldn't have been a way like

any other to win her. On the contrary, this will annoy you at first: that her treasure wouldn't need a key. She'll listen to you piously, who knows how many other saints' misfortunes they had told her. Even so, you'll decide at the last minute to frighten her, as long as you don't acknowledge that she had you. You look like someone who is in danger & isn't going to make it. You will get an infection. How does a *frittata* sound to you?"

"He nodded, crying," the friar said, in conclusion, while beating the eggs.

He was actually crying in his plate, recalling: "If not vanity, what is it, love? If not love, then what could it be?"

He wasn't looking for someone to talk to after so much silence, but rather someone to whom he could say: "I haven't talked to anyone in a very long time!" A loud fart from the friar startled him.

"You know what? I've decided to do things differently," the friar said, dividing the *frittata* in two, "I've decided to leave for good, otherwise it will end badly; it'll end with them sending the two of us to hell for abusing symbols. God knows the extent to which we are immune to them, you and I. I've decided to help you clear away the very same altar that we raised together. Perhaps, because I like living high off the hog a little more than you do. It's an enviable recipe. We turn demons into hogs, and then we eat them. It's still raining. I'm starting to think that it will be difficult for you to go out on a boat tonight. I had set it up for dusk, not including the time it takes to get all the way down the cliff to the marina. Saint Margherita will be here soon. I'll stop her in the hall. I'll tell her that you're not feeling well. I'll see about postponing it until tomorrow evening. As for her, when she hears petty lies, she usually doesn't deign to reply; she prefers to vanish, to take her revenge elsewhere. I'll reveal myself more than necessary, like kicks in the face, and I'll be with you in a matter of seconds, to help you finish putting on your make-up. I want little girls turned upside down. Far from dissuading you from it."

Now that they'd come to an agreement, they were eating in earnest. One thing was strange, and even worse, it was new: in the situations that took place in the past, and that, like this one, were thorny, the friar had opposed him to the bitter end, even after having had coffee, and, a far cry from leaving, he had settled himself forcefully under the bed, jeopardizing all his follies, unravelling in laughter any plot of degradation, curling up his lip in a sacrilegious near insult, and repudiating him in any and every way, possible or not, regardless. He'd placed a small mirror above his little altar, representing a god who would grant, flesh and blood, and banalize himself in the humblest of performances, weeping in all the most nonsensical roles, &, last but not least, in the role of himself. Martyred following a recipe, far fiercer than those Turks of old, his face scratched, with the exception of the eyes, so he could exist, thrown onto the street from a balcony of a non-fatal second floor, so he could die every day. An Indian idol, but brought back to himself, ferociously humanized, aching, tangible, gone crazy in the urn of the monologue, an infinite quotidian. But why ruin a ruin? How to make out of that a relationship of a reflection? I create for myself a network of fake relationships; it doesn't matter if they last. I'll find others, because possessing a woman or talking with a stranger is a bit like dying young. He who is in time is young. I don't want to end up in my own hands. Would a maidservant suffice? That would more than suffice!

"If not, there's always the baker's delivery boy!" the friar said, trying to guess, "and if that one doesn't last, then there's always the baker himself!"

Yet, that man of wisdom was right. Going toward someone is like going to heaven. Play his game! Whoever's game it is isn't important. We'll have a good time, and he'll win. Who is he? He has but one name, only to confuse us. We, on the other hand, give ourselves last names. You can do crazy things with a first and last name. I'm in your hands from here on out. Make a habit out of me. I'll show you everything in my room. We would need one night, one magical night.

"Coffee's ready!" the friar said, adding sugar, "drink it, and don't talk to me. I don't believe in the novels you write, but your diary is in order, it's in such fine form, beyond their wildest dreams, because to write about it elsewhere, you have to overrate everything. Nowadays, hagiographers are afraid of becoming doddering fools without prestige. Drink up! I, too, am in complete disarray. So, instead, I want my makeup to be perfect. A single technical incident in the undertaking would suffice, & that would be that. We could, however, also have written another 30 pages!"

They'd cleared the table & stacked the dirty plates on the table. "You can't tell her anything about yourself, got it," the friar said to him, a little nervous. "But, of course, of course," he said, stammering while pouring the cognac. They drank the whole bottle, standing, near the windows, watching the rain thin out and the black sky lose its color. "It's never enough!" the scandalized monk said, clinging to the neck of a new bottle. "Imagine you're about to move to a village, is that clear? Don't try to serve yourself any more, otherwise it'll end like with the Turk, you remember, the one from Lake Como, when you hoped he would be your alibi, the one who left the next day. Don't play the Elizabethan, taking her to bed in the daytime, when you know full well that her masters may come looking for her. Take her when she has free time, or at night, when they're sleeping. Don't damage her in any way. Not because you care about her in particular, but, how to say this, because you developed a conscience around collective responsibility. So, don't tell anyone, not even yourself. After all, it's like going back to the beginning, but with less judgment and without hesitations. You're a ring that encircles another ring. Just try not to make a knot out of them that will interfere with the general plan. It's a matter of time, got it? Because you have to be told things a hundred times before they sink in; but you look like you're sufficiently well-rehearsed. I have faith that this time it will really be over for you!"

"Ha, ha, ha! Stop right there, father! I'll die of laughter if you keep going on like this!"

Who knows why he laughed this time, and, what's more, it was a boisterous laugh. "Come on, do you really think that an encounter with a girl, a maidservant, will be decisive for me? I'm starting to think that you've lost your mind. But even now I'm devoutly kneeling before myself. One thing can drive away another. I don't remember anymore. These are today's wounds, and they are almost healed over. Do you ever get distracted while praying? Has that ever happened to you? It often happens to me. Now there's a girl walking by. Now she's gone. Or the butcher's father walks by. Other times, it's me, in the flesh. We ended up talking about stupidities until evening, if that's what we wanted. It's not raining anymore. The clouds are gone. You can go on that boat ride with the Saint in my place."

"That remains to be seen," the friar was saying, amusedly, "that remains to be seen." The other bottle was empty, too, but both of them could hold their liquor. They didn't get cleaned up. They approached the bathroom sink in front of the big mirror, and like two thieves, started to put on their make-up. Naturally, the friar had no reflection. As opposed to the other one, who could be seen easily: at that moment he was redoing his eyes, while having a lot of fun at the idea of what sort of monstrous mask the friar would end up with, if he were blind.

"I can see!" he said, sneering, "I can see! I'm covering up two scratches on my cheeks; what a shame that you can't see me!" Now he was addressing him informally. He was excitedly staring at himself: "I have a mouth that you, who are, nevertheless capable of anything, never succeeded in kissing!" He was being mean. Letting the monk think: "If only you could see just how ridiculous you look with that black mark on your forehead," he was saying: "Keep still, keep still, let me do it, I'll do it," and, instead of eliminating that trifle, he painted his entire nose green. "If only you could see now!" he said, deceiving him. Then, with a little sponge, he washed his nose and proceeded. "With all that rigor of yours," he said, humiliating himself, "if I weren't here to put your make-up on, you would've died of hunger by this time!" Or: "Is it really in your best interest to destroy everything, when it takes you so long to put on your make-up?" Or even, if only half his face was painted: "Since you're a big talker this evening, you'll go out like this!"

For a long time now, he would turn his pride into a friar, who, at first, mistreated him, and then a little later, humiliated, cast aside, returned from who knows where. And, also because friars are good cooks.

Saint Margherita was waiting for him in the hall. Had he really embarked upon that undertaking? In any case, he went to greet her, kissing her dress, saying: "Signora..." The Saint, indignant, recoiled from him and asked: "What's wrong now? How is it that you're not ready? It was this evening, isn't that right?"

"No, no... I'm not myself..." he said, lying like a complete idiot, "look, Signora, he isn't feeling well. I'm afraid that it won't be possible this evening... the doctor..." "The doctor?" the Saint asked, disgusted. "The doctor, Signora, the doctor... he prescribed bed rest; he can't even get out of bed, is what the doctor said... I'm here to keep him company...!" "You can go now, my good man!" the Saint said, granting him leave, "as you can see, I did the right thing in coming; I'll heal him in no time." Then, looking him right in the face: "Where does it hurt?" she asked. "I'm fine..." he said, insistently, persisting in kissing her dress. "I only hope that you'll die, you coward!" the Saint said, going to the window. "I stopped the storm, so that you could get some fresh air. Or do you think that it stopped on its own?" She looked in the distance for a long time. Then, as if she'd made up her mind, "At least tell him that I'm here!" she said, pleading with him. "I care about him," the guardian said, "don't ask this of me. Your presence could upset him. Come back tomorrow." The Saint didn't reply, but said, "Fool!" & she left.

Relieved, he went to his room. He rummaged around in an old crate and pulled out handfuls & handfuls of fake jewels, pearls, sapphires, emeralds, amethysts, rubies, mother of pearl, topaz, onyx, turquoise, agates, opals, diamonds, selenite, chrysoprase, beryllium, jades, alexandrite, lapis lazuli, carnelians, turquoise, odds & ends from old theater props. He decked himself out in necklaces, bracelets, rings, &, arriving at his urn's glass panes, holding his breath, he reclaimed his destiny next to the other martyrs, on display for public viewing.

Today, a Sunday crowd. The local inhabitants would've gone so far as to give their lives for the aqueduct to start working again. But the invaders, by this point ready to pull up stakes, were rushing to see everything there was to see, and everything that wasn't worth seeing in the town.

Their mouths wide open, in front of his urn, the yahoos were sure to know everything, while estimating the church's riches as incalculable, and that treasure was witness to that, and estimating the mosaic of those relics as a chicken bone farce.

But she, little more than a child, the girl he'd seen that morning, revealing herself in front of him, invisible, oh, everything about her was different!

"Come over here! Look at this one with the eyes! This one is too much! He has eyes! What will they think of next, and then who knows who's hiding back there!" one of the visitors said, blaspheming.

But she was crying, "All these treasures are certainly not enough," she must've been telling herself, "to buy the peace of these poor corpses!"

Then, when she was beneath his urn, she spoke to him, inspired:

"Are you looking at me? Do you see me? Is there anything I can do for you? Tell me! I'll do anything you want..."

"Bury me!" he said, under his breath.

"Where? When?" she asked, carried away.

"This evening, 10 o'clock, at my place."

"Where do you live? Is it far?"

"Not at all! It's close to you!"

"Should I bring you anything?"

"Come dressed simply."

"Ok. How will I know it's you?"

"I'll recognize you."

"See you tonight!"

"See you tonight!"

Much to his surprise, he freed himself in a flash from all his glory. He put on a pair of pants that were within reach, and, opening wide the windows, he rushed out onto the balcony. There, opposite his place, the present version of her was at the parapet, adorned with red lilies, when the Turkish arches would deviate their course. She was talking, not to him, responding listlessly to someone unseen who was questioning her from inside. He sent her more than one inconclusive signal, gestures for which not even he possessed the secret, magical if she smiled at him. She didn't understand. He was the one who didn't understand. So, she sketched out for him how she would go down from the other side, because from up there she couldn't hear anything he said. There she goes! She went inside and now she's coming down.

He put on a white shirt and rushed to the mirror to comb his hair. His face, covered in greasepaint, didn't show a single scratch.

He drank something really strong, lit two cigarettes and skipped down the stairs on the opposite side. He crossed the courtyard. It was night. He didn't go out on the street. He looked over the small retaining wall, camouflaged within a white oleander. His heart started beating hard. He waited a quarter of an hour. And then another. It started to rain, suddenly, pouring. He rushed back up his stairs. Impossible. Maybe they weren't letting her go out. Maybe she was playing on the balcony. He'd never know. All he knew for sure was that he was back in his room. The light was on:

the monk and the Saint who were playing cards. He could've guessed.

"Let's go play somewhere else!" they said, as soon as they saw him. Then they left. He opened the window and looked between the Moorish arches. My God, he didn't even know her name! He thoroughly searched a little drawer, but came up empty handed. At a certain point, he decided that someone was calling up to him from the courtyard. He ran down in the rain. It was her. "Come inside!" he said to her. As soon as they reached the shelter of the veranda: "Why did it take you so long to get here?" he asked. Then he pushed her into the kitchen. She was truly beautiful. Out of his mind from his self-assurance: "You're soaking wet, my child!" he said to her, "come on, come on, first, let's get you out of these wet clothes," and he took them off, asking: "You must be cold, aren't you?" He grabbed a towel and dried her off everywhere. "Now, let's get rid of this wet rag, too! Walk around a bit, let me see you, we wouldn't want you to catch cold, would we?" She was naked and let herself be tended to. "Now you'll feel like a new woman," he said to her, "you can't imagine how much better it feels to walk around naked at home, especially when it's raining outside. I'm taking off my clothes, too, you see?"

His clothes were off in no time flat. She was speechless. She was either nodding or smiling. "Now, you dry me off, but with your hands!" he said to her. She did as he asked. Then, as if drawn to the pile of dirty dishes, she went to the sink and started sloshing around the remaining sauce in the bottom of the pasta bowls with her hands. "There's no water," he thought, "but what difference does that make? She certainly didn't come here to wash the dishes!" He came up to her from behind. He took her in his arms, pressing on her belly with his fingers. So, then she bent down even further, willing, determined to wash the plates with her tongue. He took her like that, twice, one right after the other. Then he moved away from her. She was still a little out of breath, her thighs streaked with blood all the way down to her ankles, her breasts and face drowned in the sink's swill. He moved closer to her again and pulled her head up out of the sauce by her blond hair. With a sponge and a dish towel, he scrubbed her face & her chest. "Let's go to my room," he said, pulling her along by the hand behind him. "Do you know that it's unwise to stay here in the kitchen? For you, that is. It's a good thing that you have the Moorish villa in front of you: let's say that the folks at your place were looking for you, from here you can see them, can't you?" Then he placed her at the balcony, positioning himself almost on top of her. "You can lean over further, if you like, don't worry, I'm here to catch you!"

She was balancing herself, as if a cord from her belly against the windowsill, her feet in the air, while he was looking for the Moorish villa in her hair, disheveling the domes and the arches, just barely painted by the fresh moon, when the rubbed reds would seem as though freckles on the skin whiter than the domes, in the illusion.

It was perfect like that, if that piece of architecture opposite had been made for it to be imagined, like when we laugh in love, where the game titillates exhausted passion, to be the only one to be on one's mind, an erroneous manner, like any other, to tell yourself that it's not over.

"Oh, hands in velvet gloves!" his hands were thinking, caressing a ball of meat. "My true homeland, truly copied from a passing fancy, this beautiful Italian girl of mine bends into a serenade of moans at your cold feet, because your small towns are nomadic cells of sugar, destined to melt on the tongue of all the mute children!"

At the bottom of the shallow sea's water, black, invented by the full moon, the Moorish villa was waxing sentimental a tangle of seaweed caught on something more than a charm.

He was looking for the palm trees in her hair. He detached himself from her forcefully, as if in birth, forgetting for a moment that she was still precariously balancing herself on the windowsill. A little after that, he laid her down, half-dead, on the bed, covering her with a clean sheet. Comforted by the idea of

a rose, absorbed in a watery, red spot, which expand-
ed in the hollow of a plowed fold between her open
thighs, while looking at the sea, he started to tell her
about himself. But about himself, not about his past
life. He would've told her about his future, by starting
from here. A knight belonging to a mysterious order,
one day he decided to try his fortune and broke his
lance in two, in order to extract from it a magic wand
to throw into the lake. Disarmed and disarming, he
began turning himself round and round. It was more
than brandishing a donkey's jawbone.

When he was a child, a monk had taught him that
injustice and enemies do not exist. Since everything
is a vast pine grove! At present, and senselessly, he
could regret having embittered the Saint in this way,
&, afterwards, ask himself in which place of heaven
would Margherita find herself, with whom would she
be talking about him at that moment, and be jealous
of them, and like that go find her. Leaving that unat-
tended body rolled up in a white linen sheet, dressing himself as best as he could, sliding all the way
down to the courtyard, continuing to narrate: "... I
approached the stables. The Saint's embroidered garments were hanging on the missing door..." He ran
inside as if tearing down a wall. There she was across
from him pretending to be focused, as she'd been in
the past, half-dressed, and rubbing her stomach with
a handkerchief. Bewildered by a stack of straw that

was twitching, surely animated by some secret, he undid that ambiguous bulge with a kick and found buried there all the dirty, used bandages that he'd thrown away. "Look at the fly, look at the fly," the Saint said, her face drained of color, who had reclaimed her own countenance. "Don't act like an idiot!" the Saint said, astonished, while getting dressed in front of him, "fasten this for me here." That much was clear. In love, that fairy understood that she'd benefit more by being "her." Then, having concluded the intercourse, she became herself again. But it was precisely with "her" that everything had ended. Instead, he must've still been in love, since he couldn't find peace, not even with the servant.

"Where is that girl?!" the Saint asked, yelling and slapping him in the face. "Upstairs..." he said, closing his eyes, "... she's upstairs, on the bed, in my room; she doesn't feel well!" "Whether she feels well or not, they've come to take her away!" the Saint said. "Take her away?!" he asked, imploringly, & becoming truly suspicious.

At a flick of the Saint's hand, the exhumed bandages became animated, though vertically, as if they were white snakes, transforming themselves into a white horse and a knight. Dressed in all white, the knight looked like him, it was him, it was he who was no longer himself. On the threshold of the stables, the servant, wrapped up in the sheet, trembling, was now thrown into relief. The knight lifted her up & eased her onto the saddle and, spurring on the horse, disappeared.

"Let them go!" the Saint said, seeing that he was worried, "You'll see; they'll be back. They won't get far. They don't have enough money!"

The castellans & the maidservants belong to those who decided to stay, those who won't ever leave. That idiot thought he could leave, bringing her along with him, and yet, I'll catch up to them.

He rudely pushed aside the Saint, flying to return to his room. He was insane. He gathered up all the money there was in the house, a lot of money, & put it in a bag that he fastened to his waist. He took down from the wall a suit of armor, made entirely of iron, and dressed himself in it. He lowered the visor and went out to the street. It was dawn; the street lights lining the coast were still on. He slowly strode majestically, heavily, in the middle of the street. The drowsy carts brushed against him with their dog and their lantern, and the colonists asleep on the bier.

He would never catch up to those two on horseback. He felt like he was going to faint inside the iron. His body kept on going, dragging along his feet, like a sum of vigils, traversing the sea's proscenium.

When he was in the town square, he crashed, his face on the ground. They found him a little bit later. No one recognized him, because, when he fell, the visor had disfigured his face.

Go to sleep! Let's change the flowers! Margherita, oh, back then you were a field of chamomile, when the summer slept, her last summer, unless it wasn't, in any event, even without me, of chamomile a field, a sweet sleep of a Junoesque summer, ventilated by the wing of a migraine & invariably overcome, since the head came last, but also the last to fall. Go to sleep! If only she'd had more patience! Go to sleep! The head is mine, though it's not mine. Here it is in the reliquary, in the drops of blood of the petals redder than the most magnificent geraniums, in the cellar where nothing spoils, or it's illusion. Or, it's just in my head. Go to sleep! That idiot thought he could leave. He left and he likes flowers. He has no head, but he thinks about her anyway, because they don't live together. He stopped in a field of chamomile & poppies, and this thought would suffice... Go to sleep! We'll never catch up to those two on horseback. They'll stop at the trunk of she who is waiting, or is simply waiting for flowers. Dearest, I still have time... a bouquet of spring in the neck... for now this, & then there'll be the renovation; our love will be the color of smoke, precise, artisanal, spared from the inaccuracies of art. Florence was never a maritime republic, and that says it all.

We're sleeping. I don't even know your name. "She's sleeping!" he thought. "She's crazy!" "Go to sleep, go to sleep!" he said, whispering perverse. "So, you didn't hear what will be!"... "Go to sleep!"... The day was breaking.

That idiot thought he could leave, taking her away with him. He who catches up to them is valiant. Go to sleep! He looked outside, the lights still on, staring first at her on the bed, then at the empty bed, walking backwards ad infinitum, he bumped into the work table and, just to rest, at least a little, he sat down & wrote: "... The headlights again, the moments of a cold night, when the heart is an agitated swallow between your branches..."

A rainy morning, the arches as if a straight line of swallows, wings open the animated double arched windows, the Moorish villa was leaving. It repatriates where there are other flocks of folly, authenticating itself while stuck in one of Tunis's working-class streets, an unaware dwelling of exceptional ordinary events. It is leaving, floating on the water, corroded by Western objections, a wandering sanctuary in search of priests who would always invent it, oblivious to the African public.

There where it touches the shore, overseas, is naturally where it will remain, as if it had never been detached from it. And the Turks would live there cheaply. Go to sleep, let's change the flowers. If I weren't a building, they might believe me.

"Flora! Flora!" a voice said from between the arches. He looked up on high. She was there among the red lilies, inside a dress that was shaking a rug. Speechless, he followed her as she went back inside. She was at the window, a sign that she'd already gotten up. Feeling ashamed of himself, *&* not, for keeping her in bed a little longer, it nearly happened that he silently, only as much as not to be heard, it nearly happened that he called out to her:

"Signorina...!"

"They're awake, Flora... get dressed *&* go!" he said softly, while uncovering the abandoned sheet.

There was no Flora. Or she got dressed and left.

COLOPHON

OUR LADY OF THE TURKS
was handset in InDesign CC.

The text font is *Skolar*.
The display font is *Boita*.

Book design *&* typesetting: Alessandro Segalini
Cover image: Federico Gori
Cover design: Alessandro Segalini *&* CMP

OUR LADY OF THE TURKS
is published by Contra Mundum Press.

Contra Mundum Press   New York · London · Melbourne

CONTRA MUNDUM PRESS

Dedicated to the value & the indispensable importance of the individual voice, to works that test the boundaries of thought & experience.

The primary aim of Contra Mundum is to publish translations of writers who in their use of form and style are *à rebours*, or who deviate significantly from more programmatic & spurious forms of experimentation. Such writing attests to the volatile nature of modernism. Our preference is for works that have not yet been translated into English, are out of print, or are poorly translated, for writers whose thinking & æsthetics are in opposition to timely or mainstream currents of thought, value systems, or moralities. We also reprint obscure and out-of-print works we consider significant but which have been forgotten, neglected, or overshadowed.

There are many works of fundamental significance to *Weltliteratur* (& *Weltkultur*) that still remain in relative oblivion, works that alter and disrupt standard circuits of thought — these warrant being encountered by the world at large. It is our aim to render them more visible.

For the complete list of forthcoming publications, please visit our website. To be added to our mailing list, send your name and email address to: info@contramundum.net

Contra Mundum Press
P.O. Box 1326
New York, NY 10276
USA

OTHER CONTRA MUNDUM PRESS TITLES

SOME FORTHCOMING TITLES

THE FUTURE OF KULCHUR
A PATRONAGE PROJECT

LEND CONTRA MUNDUM PRESS (CMP) YOUR SUPPORT

With bookstores and presses around the world struggling to survive, and many actually closing, we are forming this patronage project as a means for establishing a continuous & stable foundation to safeguard our longevity. Through this patronage project we would be able to remain free of having to rely upon government support &/or other official funding bodies, not to speak of their timelines & impositions. It would also free CMP from suffering the vagaries of the publishing industry, as well as the risk of submitting to commercial pressures in order to persist, thereby potentially compromising the integrity of our catalog.

CAN YOU SACRIFICE $10 A WEEK FOR KULCHUR?

For the equivalent of merely 2–3 coffees a week, you can help sustain CMP and contribute to the future of kulchur. To participate in our patronage program we are asking individuals to donate $500 per year, which amounts to $42/month, or $10/week. Larger donations are of course welcome and beneficial. All donations are tax-deductible through our fiscal sponsor Fractured Atlas. If preferred, donations can be made in two installments. We are seeking a minimum of 300 patrons per year and would like for them to commit to giving the above amount for a period of three years.

Part tax-deductible donation, part exchange, for your contribution you will receive every CMP book published during the patronage period as well as 20 books from our back catalog. When possible, signed or limited editions of books will be offered as well.

Your contribution will help with basic general operating expenses, yearly production expenses (book printing, warehouse & catalog fees, etc.), advertising and outreach, and editorial, proofreading, translation, typography, design and copyright fees. Funds may also be used for participating in book fairs and staging events. Additionally, we hope to rebuild the *Hyperion* section of the website in order to modernize it.

From Pericles to Mæcenas & the Renaissance patrons, it is the magnanimity of such individuals that have helped the arts to flourish. Be a part of helping your kulchur flourish; be a part of history.

To lend your support & become a patron, please visit the subscription page of our website: contramundum.net/subscription

For any questions, write us at: info@contramundum.net